SKYONFIRE

EMMY LAYBOURNE

SKYONFIRE

*Hodder
Children's
Books*

HODDER CHILDREN'S BOOKS

First published in the US in 2013 by Feiwel and Friends, an imprint of Macmillan
First published in Great Britain in 2013 by Hodder Children's Books
This edition published in 2017 by Hodder and Stoughton

4

A CIP catalogue record for this book
is available from the British Library.

ISBN 978 1 444 91472 6

Typeset in Goudy Old Style and Akzidenz Grotesque by
Avon DataSet Ltd, Bidford-on-Avon, Warwickshire
Printed and bound in Great Britain
by Clays Ltd, St Ives plc

The paper and board used in this book
are made from wood from responsible sources

Hodder Children's Books
An imprint of
Hachette Children's Group
Part of Hodder and Stoughton
Carmelite House
50 Victoria Embankment
London EC4Y 0DZ

An Hachette UK Company
www.hachette.co.uk

www.hachettechildrens.co.uk

Still for Sam

To whoever finds this:

Here's a math problem for you.

Eight kids who cannot be exposed to the air for longer than 30—40 seconds without experiencing horrible, really psychotic consequences set out to travel 67 miles down a dark highway in a school bus that survived a freak hailstorm and crashing through the plate-glass window of a Greenway superstore. The kids are likely to be attacked or detained by an unknown quantity of obstacles including chemically deranged murderers, highway robbers, roadblocks, and other unforseen complications.

Calculate the odds of their arrival to the Denver International Airport, where, they believe, they will be rescued.

I know, you're missing data so you cannot really calculate the odds properly. But if you know anything about math — even the most basic principles of odds and probability — you know this: Our odds suck.

That's why I'm writing this letter. So when you find this, you will know who was here.

On the bus with me are:

Niko Mills — Our leader. He is (or was) a junior at Lewis Palmer High. He's also a Boy Scout and has type A blood, which means that if he's exposed to the air for more than a minute, he will start to blister and die.

Brayden Cutlass — Junior. Type AB, so will suffer

from paranoid delusions but that hardly matters —
he's nearly unconscious. He's the reason, well, one of
the reasons, why we're trying to get to Denver. He was
shot in the shoulder by one of the two outsiders we
allowed to enter the Greenway with us. The hospital in
Monument is closed, but we have been told there are
doctors at DIA, because that's where the evacuations
are taking place.

Josie Miller — Sophomore. Also type AB. One of
the nicest girls I have ever met, not that that matters,
but just in case someone reads this.

Sahalia Wenner — Only 13, but thinks she's in high
school. Type B, like me. We show no obvious visible
effects but will suffer from 'reproductive failure' so
that none of us can ever have a child. Big whoop.

Batiste Harrison — Second grade. Type B, like
Sahalia and me. Can be a bit preachy sometimes.
Definitely goes to church but I don't know which one.

Ulysses Dominguez — First grade. Type AB. English
not so good.

Max Skolnik — First grade. Type A. Has wild hair
and tells wild stories. Not that you could see his hair or
hear his stories now, since he's bundled up in five
layers of clothing and wearing an air mask. We all are.

That's everyone on the bus. But some of us stayed
behind. Like my stupid 16-year-old brother, Dean
Grieder.

He stayed in the Greenway on Old Denver Highway
in Monument, CO, with the following:

2

Astrid Heyman — Senior. Type O. Girl of my brother's stupid dreams who, by the way, isn't even nice and I don't think even likes my brother as a friend, much less anything else.

Chloe (can't remember her last name) — Third grader. Type O. Obnoxious.

Caroline McKinley — Kindergarten and

Henry McKinley — Kindergarten. They're twins. Type AB.

If you have found this notebook, please, please go and rescue my brother and the others. They could still be waiting in the Greenway for help.

Dean says he stayed because he, Astrid, and Chloe are all type O and will turn into bloodthirsty monsters if they're exposed to the chemicals, but we were going to tie them up and sedate them. They would have been fine.

There. Now there's a record of my brother's bad decision. Though I guess if you are fishing this out of the charred hulk of our bus and are about to go rescue him, then maybe he made the right choice after all.

I also want to mention Jake Simonsen. Senior. Type B. Though he abandoned our group while out on a reconnaissance mission, he deserves to be listed here, because he was one of the original Monument 14.

That's it for now.

Alex Grieder — Age 13. Type B.

September 28, 2024

1 DEAN

I T WAS A LOVELY moment. Astrid hugging little
Caroline and Henry. Luna barking and licking all the
faces she could reach.

Of course, we were all wearing five layers of clothing
to protect our skin from the compounds. And I had on
my air mask. And Chloe was off to the side, masked and
layered up and lying in a drugged sleep on an inflatable
mattress. But for us, in the Greenway, it was a nice
moment.

Seeing Astrid kiss them all over their little, dirty,
freckled faces made me feel hopeful and happy. I guess
seeing Astrid expressing love for them made my
own feelings for her swell up. I felt like my heart would
burst.

Then Astrid took in a deep breath.

5

And I saw her nostrils flare. She inhaled too long and I knew the rage was kicking in.

'Why did you stay?' she moaned. 'You dumb, DUMB KIDS. WHY DID YOU STAY?'

She crushed the twins to her chest, holding one of their red-headed skulls in each hand.

And then I had to tackle her and hold her down.

So much for lovely Greenway moments.

Caroline and Henry were crying as I wrestled Astrid to the ground.

'Get her mask,' I yelled.

Astrid lashed out, pushing up against me.

Luna was barking her fluffy white head off.

'Caroline,' I hollered, my voice muffled by my mask. 'Get her air mask! Bring it here.'

Astrid had let it fall to the ground when she saw the twins and started hugging and kissing them.

Caroline brought me the mask, as Astrid kicked and bucked. It took everything I had to keep her down.

'Put it on her!' I shouted.

Caroline, crying hard, pressed the mask over Astrid's face. Henry came over and helped her hold it in place.

'Stop fighting me!' I yelled at Astrid. 'You're okay. You just got a hit of the compounds. Just breathe.'

'Do it harder,' Henry said to Caroline and she nodded. They crushed the mask down more firmly.

Astrid looked at us, at me. The fury in her sky-blue eyes receded, slowly, until finally she closed them and her whole body softened underneath me.

I stayed on top of her until she said hoarsely, 'I'm all right.'

I got to my knees, then to my feet.

Astrid put her hand up and placed it on the mask, gently pushing the twins aside as she sat up.

Caroline patted Astrid on the back.

'It's okay, we know it wasn't really you.'

'Yeah,' Henry agreed. 'It was Monster-Astrid, not Real-Astrid.'

'Come on, everyone,' I said. 'We gotta fix the gate! Now!'

We had needed to open the gate to let out the bus with Alex, Niko, Josie, and the rest of them. The layers of blankets and plastic and plywood we'd used to seal the gate and make the store airtight were all messed up now.

First we had to reseal the gate and then, somehow, purify the air. Would the entire store be contaminated now? I didn't know.

I grabbed the blankets and plastic sheeting that hung from the gate and pressed them back into place. 'Hand me a staple gun!' I shouted to the twins.

The staple guns were still there, set to the side, from the first time we'd sealed the gate. I was now glad we were so sloppy as to leave our tools around. Or maybe Niko had left them there on purpose. He was very thorough that way.

I got the blankets and plastic back up in the time it took for Astrid to get to her feet and drag the first

7

plywood sheet over.

I tried to staple it but only got three good hits when there was a hollow CLINK-CLINK sound from the staple gun. I was out of staples.

'Shoot,' I mumbled.

There weren't any extra staples in the box, either.

'Be right back!' I hollered.

You had to shout to be understood in the stupid air masks.

I didn't want to think about Niko and Josie, and Alex trying to communicate through them on the bus.

They should never have left and every time it even came into my mind that they had left, I got angry.

I didn't need to be angry just then, though. I needed to be smart. We had to get the store sealed up quickly.

I headed to Home Improvement.

I passed Chloe on her air mattress. She still had her mask on and all her layers and was totally out cold. The sleeping pill Niko had given her was strong.

She was going to be so pissed off when she woke up and discovered that Niko and the rest had gone on without her.

She had missed the whole drama of Astrid and me telling everyone we weren't going. That it wasn't safe for us to go out, because of our blood type.

She certainly hadn't been consulted when Niko took her off the bus.

But we were right, I told myself. It *was* too dangerous

for us to go out there. Astrid had gotten just a momentary whiff of the compounds and had gone berserk. Us out in the open air, trying to make it sixty miles to Denver? We would have murdered them.

I was sure of it. We made the right choice.

And we had enough supplies in the Greenway to last us for weeks or months. Long enough for the others to make it to DIA and arrange some kind of a rescue. Or long enough to wait out the compounds – we had heard the effects would only last for three to six months . . .

As I got back with my reloaded staple gun, I saw that Caroline and Henry were gently bouncing next to Chloe's slumbering form on the air mattress. Luna was curled up next to them.

They looked like three little aliens and their pet dog, out to sea on a raft.

Then there came a loud THUNK from the gate.

Astrid jumped and looked at me.

The THUNK came again.

'Hey!' came a voice.

'Hello?' Astrid yelled.

'I knew it! I knew I saw a light! Hey, Jeff, I was right! There's somebody in there!'

'Who are you?' I shouted.

'Name's Scott Fisher. Open the gate and let us in, would ya?'

'Sorry,' I lied. 'We can't open it.'

'Oh, sure, you can. You just did. It was just open a minute ago. We saw the light! Come on!'

DAY 12

'Yeah! Let us in,' echoed another voice. Jeff, I presumed.

'Dude, you have to let us in. It's like an emergency out here!'

Dur.

'Yeah, I know,' I said. 'But we can't.'

'Well, why the hell not?' he demanded.

Astrid came next to me.

'Because we let two grown-ups in before and one of them molested a girl and tried to shoot our leader!' she shouted through her mask.

'Well, now we're not like that. We're real nice.'

'Sorry,' Astrid said. She patted the plywood and nodded for me to nail it.

'Come on!' he yelled. 'We're thirsty and hungry. People are dying out here! Let us in.'

'Sorry,' I yelled.

I shot a staple in.

Scott and Jeff rattled the gate some and cursed a fair amount, but by the time we got the rest of the plywood back up, we could hardly hear them.

I was examining the wall, and had made up my mind to add another layer of plastic sheeting, after we got the purifiers running, when Astrid tugged on my arm.

'While we're all geared up, let's go throw some food down to that guy from the roof.'

'What?' I asked.

'Let's throw them down some food and water!' she yelled.

'Why?' I asked.

She shrugged.

'We have so much and they have nothing. We should help them.'

Aargh, I didn't want to go up on the roof. Not at all.

I was exhausted and I wanted to get the air purifiers set up.

But Astrid stood there looking at me like it was obviously a good idea. Like it was obviously the right thing to do.

'I want to get air purifiers set up, first,' I argued.

'Me and the kids will do that,' she yelled through her mask. 'You should take the food up while the guys are still outside.'

'But–'

I couldn't think straight enough to tell her why it wasn't a good idea. Maybe she'd think I was lazy or scared to go on the roof or something.

'All right,' I said. 'I'll do it.'

She turned toward the kids without even, I don't know, saying thanks.

'Caroline and Henry,' she called. 'Grab a cart and come with me.'

'Wait,' I said. 'First we get the purifiers running. Then I take the food.'

Astrid looked at me and sighed.

Okay, it's hard to read expressions through the plastic visor of an industrial face mask, but what I read in her expression went something like:

Ah, this dumb kid feels like he's getting pushed

DAY 12

around so he's taking a stand on a small, insignificant detail. But I guess if he needs to win this little victory for the sake of his pride, then I will give in.

Then she said, 'Fine, but let's hurry.'

We had eight different models of air purifiers in the Greenway and four to six units of each. Astrid and I set up the larger ones, and Caroline and Henry were in charge of putting the smaller ones around the store.

We used a lot of extension cords, as most of the outlets were on the walls.

I headed to the Pizza Shack. We had moved all the food into the big refrigerators there when we realized we'd be staying for a while.

I grabbed some EZ cans of tuna and a bunch of old bread and some fibre breakfast bars no one liked and some horrible Popsicles not even the least discriminating of our kids would eat. And a couple gallons of store-brand lemonade.

I threw the stuff into an empty plastic storage bin that was sitting around from before and carried it back to the storeroom.

We'd been alone in the store for all of two hours and already she was bossing me around as if I were some little kid or something. Not good.

Holding the tub in my arms, I entered the storeroom backward, nudging the doors open with my back.

I turned and nearly dropped the tub.

I was so wrapped up in thinking about Astrid I had forgotten about the bodies.

It was bloody back there. Robbie's body lay half off the air mattress. The air had mostly gone out of the mattress, so his bloody corpse was just lying on a flattish rubber mat. The blanket we'd thrown over top of him was saturated with blood in a couple of places.

Just beyond him lay Mr Appleton, who had died in his sleep. A more peaceful way to go, to be sure. As if to prove it, his air mattress was still pleasantly inflated.

The outsiders who had come and torn our group apart were now dead in the storeroom.

I hadn't had time to really think about Robbie and the way he betrayed us.

He and Mr Appleton had come to the store and we had let them in. But when it came time for them to leave, Robbie hadn't wanted to. Mr Appleton fell ill and then, later that night, we had found Robbie with Sahalia.

In the scuffle, Brayden had been shot and Robbie had been killed.

Mr Appleton died later in the night. There wasn't much we could have done to change that, I don't think.

But Robbie ...

I could have looked at Robbie there and been angry. As far as I understood it, he had tried to get Sahalia to sleep with him. Whether by force or by manipulation, I'm not sure. But he showed his true colours and they were disgusting. A, like, fifty-year-old man with a thirteen-

DAY 12

year-old? Disgusting. We thought he was a loving father-type guy and he turned out to be a letch.

And if Robbie hadn't assaulted Sahalia, Brayden would still be okay. Niko and Alex and the rest wouldn't have had to try to make it to Denver.

But I just felt sad.

Robbie and Mr Appleton were just two more people dead from this chain of disasters.

The little kids knew nothing about what had happened and I had to keep it that way.

I added 'Hide the bodies' to my mental list of things to do.

After I fed the stupid strangers outside the store.

The hatch to the roof was easy to unlock. Niko had fixed sheeting over it with Velcro, so you could just rip it open and it would hang off to the side. And the padlock had the key right in it.

I set the bin down on the step in front of me and pushed the hatch up and open.

The last time I'd been on this roof we hadn't known anything about the compounds. We had watched the cloud going up from NORAD, thirty miles away.

The last time I'd been on this roof I tried to kill my brother.

It was dark now. The air seemed to absorb the light seeping out from the hatch. The sky above was opaque black. No stars. No clouds. Just black mud suspended in the air.

I cursed myself for not bringing a flashlight.

I didn't want to go all the way back for one, though, so what I did was set the box down on the roof and scooted it toward the edge, crawling behind it.

I sure as hell didn't want to fall off the roof in the dark.

After a minute of undignified crawling and scooting, the bin came up against the edge of the roof. I tipped it up and over and listened to it come crashing down.

'Hey!' I heard Scott Fisher yell.

'You're welcome!' I hollered.

They'd find the loot. And I'd be inside by the time they did.

They were lucky Astrid had a nice streak in her and that I was such a pushover.

I edged my way back toward the light coming from the hatch. I couldn't wait to take the air mask off.

The whole mask/glasses combo was driving me crazy. The mask was large enough to fit over my glasses, but it made them cut into the bridge of my nose. And my nose was still battered from when Jake had beat me up, so that hurt. A lot.

And I wanted to get my layers off. The layers were starting to bunch up under my arms and behind my knees.

Again, I tried not to think about Alex and Niko and the rest.

They had sixty miles to cover, wearing their layers and air masks, on a half-fixed school bus on a dangerous and

DAY 12

dark highway. And I was whining to myself about a couple of hours in layers and a mask.

I got to my feet and started to make my way, slowly, back toward the hatch. In a dark world, that leaked light looked really bright, I tell you.

But I went slowly, because the roof was uneven and dented in places from the hailstorm a million years ago that had landed us safely in the Greenway.

I was thinking about the hailstorm and about how lucky we were that the grade-school bus driver, Mrs Wooly, had not only thought to drive the bus into the store to get the little kids out of the hail, but had then returned to rescue us high school kids. I was thinking about Mrs Wooly and wondering what had happened to her in the end. Had she made it to safety? Had she even thought about returning for us, as she promised, or had she just decided to fend for herself?

I was thinking about Mrs Wooly when the light from the hatch went out.

I was alone, on the roof, in the dark.

2 ALEX

THIS IS SLOW GOING.

In 3 hours, we have gone approximately 8 miles.

Denver International Airport is more than 60 miles away.

This is going to take longer than I had hoped. It took us 20 minutes just to get from the Greenway parking lot onto I-25.

It's hard to see out of the windows because of the Plexiglas, which is not clear like regular glass. It's like driving through fog.

The highway is cracked in places. Sometimes there are gaps and craters in the asphalt. But so far there's been nothing the bus couldn't make it over.

Every 200 yards or so, there are big, battery-powered floodlights. These are good:

1. They lead the way.
2. They help us to see better as we pass.

61 MILES

3. They give us hope that there's someone looking out
    for us.

There are cars densely packed on each side of the highway and just one lane going through the middle. My best guess is that the military came along and cleared a path through. In some places, cars have just been lifted up and pushed on their sides to make room.

The cars are not what is scary, of course. Nobody would just get scared in a long, weird parking lot like the I-25.

It's the bodies.

We see them, dead where they were crawling out of their cars.

Some are just bloody messes – they must have been type A, like Niko and Max.

In some cars, as we pass by, our headlights shine on slick black liquid splashed all over the inside of the car. It's blood. I guess those people were type A, too. Or maybe those cars had two people in them, a type O and something else, and the O just ripped them apart or something.

The other thing that's scary is the white mould.

There is a kind of white foamy substance growing up over the car tyres and up onto the bodies of the cars.

It looks almost like the car tyres have frozen, with snowdrifts of ice particles covering them, but we had to drive through some of it at one point and it didn't seem like ice when we drove through. It seemed wet and dense, like mould.

I think it's a rubber-eating fungus.

Anyway, it explains why we're not seeing more cars out driving.

Only tyres that have been kept out of the air aren't covered in the mould.

We just drove over a body lying right in the road. The thumps were sick and though we couldn't *hear* them over the engine, we could *feel* them. The body had a heavy give to it as we went over it.

A meaty, heavy give, if that even makes sense.

These are the kinds of things I get to think about, Dean, while you are lazing about in the Greenway, eating Whitman's Sampler chocolates with Astrid and Chloe and the twins.

Max, Ulysses, and Batiste are sitting crammed together in one double seat. It's a funny sight to me – behind them there are all these containers filled with food, boxes with gallons of water – all these supplies jammed in a big jumble, and then in front of the mess are these three boys, all padded up, wearing masks. And they're playing Matchbox cars.

I guess one of them (probably Max) stashed the cars in his backpack. And now they're having races on the seat back in front of them and crashing the cars and making those car-driving noises little boys make.

Sahalia is with Brayden in the front seat.

He's in bad shape.

Sahalia keeps saying urgent things to Niko and Josie and me about Brayden. Probably things like *He's weak. He's grey. He looks like he's going to die.* But we can't really hear her.

That's because of the air masks. They make it almost impossible to hear, over the engine noise and the sound of our own heartbeats hammering in our ears.

I think Sahalia's crying under her mask.

* * *

61 MILES

(later)

Right before Castle Rock, there was a long stretch of open highway ('open' meaning that there was one clear lane with no obstacles to go around).

We got up to 20 miles an hour, which felt like flying.

I laughed and I think Niko was grinning under his mask, but I could only tell by the corner of his eye that I could see.

Josie was smiling and she turned and gave me a big thumbs-up. She looked funny – we all did – with her five layers of sweatpants and sweatshirts and then a large orange slicker on top of it all. But she looked hopeful and I smiled at her and gave her thumbs-up back.

When Josie was happy, it made everyone happy. And this made sense, because she was like the mom of the group. Everyone depended on her for her good, easy way of being.

Max came up and asked Josie to make him some lunch.

'We're hungry!' he shouted.

'You'll have to wait, honey!' Josie shouted back.

'But we're hungry!'

Josie took Max by the hand and led him to the back of the bus. She was trying to tell him it was too dangerous to remove his mask to eat when Sahalia screamed.

Brayden had slumped to the floor.

Sahalia was screaming his name and pulling at his body, trying to lug him back onto the seat, I guess.

Josie came back up the aisle.

'How long has he been unconscious?' Josie asked Sahalia.

Sahalia said something back but I couldn't hear what it was.

'Brayden, Brayden! You've got to stick with us!' Josie yelled. 'We're trying to get you—'

'He knows all that. I've been telling him that but then he fell asleep and you have to help him!' Sahalia was freaking out.

'Sahalia, listen to me—' Josie pleaded.

'We have to pull off and get help!' Sahalia was screeching.

'Stop screaming!' Josie shouted. She was getting mad.

Suddenly Josie pulled off her mask. Then the ski mask she'd had over it.

'I can't understand you, Sahalia,' Josie said. 'Calm down and speak more slowly.'

She was holding on to Sahalia's arms. Kindly, but firmly. That's how Josie is.

Then Sahalia took off her masks and fleece mask.

The little boys started to yell. I think they were saying something like, 'No fair'. They wanted to take their masks off, too.

I knew Sahalia was type B, like me. Type Bs suffered the least serious of the four effects – loss of sexual function.

And Josie was type AB – so unless she got her mask on soon, she would start hallucinating and accusing us all of trying to kill her or something.

'He's dying. He's dying and you two are going too slow!' Sahalia shouted.

Her eyes were red from crying and she looked thin-faced.

She was acting mad, but I have noticed that Sahalia usually acts mad, even if she's feeling something else. Like being scared or even happy.

Niko yelled something muffled from the driver's seat. Most likely something like, 'What's happening back there?'

He didn't stop driving. That was the right decision, given the circumstances. Brayden might be shot and he might be dying, but

21

61 MILES

if we didn't keep moving and get him to Denver, Brayden would die for sure, along with the rest of us.

'Brayden!' Josie said. She snuffled a little. 'Can you hear me?'

I was watching and I saw it happen.

Josie shook her head. She looked like she had a mosquito buzzing around her. She shook her head and stumbled backward onto her heels.

Josie put her hands up to her head and started laughing. Laughing mean.

'Ew,' Sahalia sniped. 'What's wrong with you?'

Then Josie lunged at Sahalia. The two of them fell into the aisle and Sahalia started screaming.

Niko stopped the bus. 'What's going on back there?' he yelled. Niko came hurrying back and grabbed Josie, trying to get her off Sahalia.

Josie wasn't AB. She was O!

Why had I thought . . . why had I been certain she was AB?

She was type O and she was trying to kill Sahalia.

'Get rope!' Niko yelled but I couldn't remember where the rope was.

The boxes were not in good order. Food was in with medical supplies and batteries were in with the tarps and I couldn't find the rope.

And all the while I was looking, the little boys were screaming and clutching one another and sobbing, and Niko was trying to drag Josie off Sahalia and I still couldn't find the rope.

Then I found it. (Under the seat in front of the little boys.)

I ripped the package open and I got the end free and by this time Josie had raked him across his face and his mask was pushed aside.

'Your mask!' I shouted.

Niko had Josie facedown in the aisle. Her face was pressed onto the floor mat and she was snarling and bucking.

He reached up and pushed the mask back over his face.

Josie elbowed him in the side of the head and tried to throw him off her.

I didn't know what to do with the rope so I just handed it to Niko.

'TIE. HER. FEET!' he shouted.

Josie kicked me in the head but I got her feet tied up.

Niko had one of her hands in his and her other was pinned under her.

He jerked her hand out from under her body and somehow got her two hands tied together. Now she couldn't do so much damage.

No matter how she writhed and raged, she couldn't get free.

Niko didn't have to tell me, I knew what we needed: the sleeping pills. It took me ages to find them. But I found a new packet of the sleeping pills and popped one out of its pouch and gave it to Niko.

He smothered it into her mouth and motioned for me to give him another. I did. A few moments later, she went still.

Sahalia still had her mask off. She was lying on the floor between the second and third seats, crying.

Niko went and helped her up.

'I thought she was type B, like me,' Sahalia said.

Niko said something that sounded like, 'We didn't know.'

'I thought she was type AB,' I said.

'She said she knew her type,' Niko told us. 'She was sure she was B.'

How could we not have known for sure? I tried to remember. I

61 MILES

guess when we'd all been exposed to the chemical warfare compounds, Josie had not been there.

Niko coughed and Sahalia leaned forward, concerned.

There was blood on the inside of his air mask.

3 DEAN

I FUMBLED TOWARD THE HATCH, feet catching on the dents from the long-ago hailstorm.

Had Astrid shut me out? No. It couldn't be that.

My heart was in my mouth and my face sweaty and cold.

Was someone up there with me? NO.

My foot tapped against the door frame. I felt down with my fingers.

The hatch was open.

The lights had just gone out below.

And then I realized how stupid we had been.

For most of the two weeks we'd been in the Greenway, we had had almost all the lights off to conserve power.

My little brother, Alex, the tech genius, had figured

DAY 12

out how to work the complicated control panel for the store's solar power system. He isolated the lighting just to the Kitchen and the Train (our makeshift bedroom in the back corner of the store). But for the last – I don't know – two or three hours the lights had been on at full power.

And we had hooked up about thirty air purifiers to the system all at once.

We were out of juice. Pure and simple.

I sealed the hatch behind me and made my way down the stairs in pitch blackness.

I edged toward the door, skirting the area with the blood and the bodies. I did *not* want to tumble onto Robbie's dead body.

They were calling for me. Astrid and Caroline and Henry, sounding frantic and scared.

'I'm here! I'm okay!' I called.

'Where are you?' Astrid yelled.

'I'll come to you,' I shouted back. 'Where are you?'

'We're in the Train!'

I was used to getting around the store in the dark, but this was different. Before there was always a glow coming from the Kitchen and the Train area. Now the whole store was pitch black.

I went first to the Automotive aisle. I knew there were some flashlights on the floor, because that was where we had been tending to Mr Appleton and Brayden before.

I found a headlamp and two flashlights and clicked them on.

As I got closer to the Train, Henry called out: 'We can see you!'

'We see your lights bouncing,' Caroline added.

'We blew the system, didn't we?' Astrid called.

I could tell from the quality of her voice that she had her mask off.

'It's safe?' I asked her, pointing to my own.

'I don't know about up front. But back here, it's okay.'

I handed her a flashlight and took my mask off. Removing my glasses for a moment, I rubbed the bridge of my nose.

'Oh, Dean,' Astrid said. 'Your face.'

Maybe she'd forgotten that I had the two black eyes. Maybe she'd also forgotten that it was her boyfriend (ex-boyfriend, I hoped), Jake, who'd given them to me.

Truth is, I deserved those black eyes, though that didn't make me feel charitable toward Jake. He was handsome and popular and charming, and when the going got tough, he had started doing drugs from the Pharmacy.

Then he wandered away when we sent him outside to find out if the hospital was up and running. Astrid deserved better.

'The power is out because we drained the solar power reserve,' I said.

The twins gasped and I rushed to reassure them, 'It's okay, it's okay. We've got lots of batteries and flashlights and there are even some lanterns. We'll be fine.'

DAY 12

'How will we cook?' asked Henry.

'There's a pretty big camping section,' I answered. 'Ever cooked over a camp stove? It's really fun.'

Suddenly there was a groan.

Astrid turned and the light caught on the form of Chloe, sitting up and pulling off her mask.

She looked around and rubbed her eyes.

'You guys,' she said menacingly, 'why am I not in Denver?'

Chloe on a good day was a handful and this was not a good day for Chloe.

She was livid.

'I am supposed to be in Denver right now, snuggling up to my nana and you tell me you kept me off the bus ON PURPOSE?'

She was really throwing a fantastic tantrum and I was sort of sad that the lights were out. I would have liked to see her red, screaming little face.

'I should be on a jet plane getting evacuated to Alaska, not trapped here with a bunch of Greenway *losers*!'

I bet the veins in her neck were standing out, like she was some three-foot-tall drill sergeant.

But, alas, I could only get a glimpse of her every once in a while, when she walked into one of the twins' flashlight beams.

Caroline and Henry did not think it was funny and they were both crying, trying to get Chloe to stop shouting.

'Chloe, please! It's better here. It's safer and it's not scary,' Henry pleaded.

'We came back, it was so scary out there!' Caroline said. 'We'll be rescued soon. You'll see.'

Astrid had retreated a while ago. She went to get more flashlights and some battery-powered lanterns. Maybe some candles, too.

I just sat on the futon couch and let Chloe rant. I figured eventually she'd either lose steam or her voice.

But then Luna started acting funny.

She jumped up, ears perked.

Her legs twitched and she gave one short bark, looking off in the direction of the front of the store, then looked up at me.

'Shhh!' I said to Chloe.

'And to think I even ever *liked* you, *Dean*!' she was yelling.

'Chloe, shut up!' I shouted. 'Look at Luna!'

And then Luna took off like a shot.

I hollered to Astrid as we followed Luna.

Luna raced toward the Kitchen.

'Who's there?' I shouted as I approached.

I tried to sound firm, but my voice broke.

She kept running into the Kitchen and barking at something behind the main counter, then running back to me.

'Who's there?'

There wasn't any sound. Not any human sound.

DAY 12

Suddenly Luna stood stock-still, one front leg pulled up into her body and her nose aimed under the stove.

'What's wrong with Luna?' Chloe screamed.

What *was* she doing? I didn't know.

'She's pointing,' Astrid said, coming at us from the direction of the Food aisles. 'Luna's just pointing. There's some kind of animal under there.'

She was *pointing*! You think about a hunting dog pointing, like a golden retriever or a Lab. Not a fluffy little puffball like our Luna.

I shined my flashlight under the stove and, sure enough, I saw two small red eyes shining back at me.

'It's a rat,' I said.

'Ew!' the kids screamed.

'Can I see it?' Chloe asked.

'Stay back,' I commanded. 'Just stay back.'

'I'll go get a trap,' Astrid said. 'Or two ... or twenty.'

'Yeah" I said. 'Good thinking.'

'Don't kill it!' Chloe protested. 'We should catch it and keep it for a pet.'

'No,' I said. 'That's a horrible idea.'

'No, it's not, *Dean*,' she spat. 'I'm going to catch him and then we can tame him and have him as a pet!' she bragged to Caroline and Henry.

'But we already have a pet. We have Luna,' Caroline objected.

'You can never have too many pets, dingball!'

'Chloe, you stay away from that rat. Astrid's bringing back a trap.'

But the little twerp went over to the counter and picked up a cardboard box full of straws and dumped them on the ground.

'Come on, I'll get it out with that broom, and, Henry, you scoop it up with this box!'

'Chloe! Get away from there!'

She just wasn't paying any attention to me at all! I went over and grabbed her arm. I didn't want to blow my top, but really, I'd had enough of her.

'You don't get to tell me what to do, you *traitor*,' Chloe yelled.

She broke out of my grip and slammed against the stove.

The rat came out, like a streak, and ran right toward Caroline. Luna barked like crazy and attacked it.

Caroline screamed and took a step back, but the rat and Luna got all tangled up with Caroline's legs, and somehow, that godforsaken rat bit Caroline.

Then, finally, Luna got that rat between her jaws and shook the life out of it.

Chloe and Henry and Caroline were all screaming. I grabbed Caroline and lifted her into my arms. She was clutching her leg.

Luna dropped the rat at my feet and sat down.

'*Bad* dog! *Bad* dog,' Chloe screamed at Luna. 'We were supposed to catch it, not kill it.'

Luna cowered away from Chloe.

'*Shut up*, Chloe,' I hollered. 'That stupid rat bit Caroline! If you'd just have left it alone, none of this

DAY 12

would have happened.'

Chloe started a different type of wailing now – a you-hurt-my-feelings kind of cry.

Luna began to lick her wounds.

'It's not my fault!' Chloe sobbed.

But it was. It totally was.

'What happened?' Astrid yelled, rushing back with the now-useless traps.

Astrid shined the way for me as I carried Caroline back to the Train.

Ther were first-aid supplies right in the living room.

The wound was small. Two sets of puncture marks. It was more of a nip than a bite, really.

I cleaned it with Bactine and applied some antibacterial ointment and a big neon-orange Band-Aid.

Caroline's freckled face was pale and tear streaked.

She and her brother were so dreamy, most of the time.

Sometimes I had the feeling that they didn't really know where they were, even, or understand how serious the situation was.

They were five years old.

Five.

'I hate rats,' she said to me quietly.

'Everyone does. They're horrible.'

'I'm glad it's dead,' she choked out.

Her face was twisted up.

'I don't care if God will be angry at me. I'm glad it's dead.'

I hugged her to me.

'God's not mad at you, Caroline,' I told her.

But I had the thought that if you were a person who believed in God, and you lived in Monument, Colorado, in the fall of '24 you really had to wonder.

We tried to clean Luna's wounds but she scooted between the back of the futon couch and the wall of the Train.

Astrid had gathered a shopping cart full of lights that ran on batteries.

To Henry's and Caroline's delight, and Chloe's, once she stopped pouting, there were some battery-powered Christmas tree lights.

Astrid let them string them up all over the walls of the Living Room.

I was rooting through the cart, trying to find batteries for the lanterns when I felt Astrid's hand on my shoulder.

'Hey,' she said.

'Hey,' I answered. I'm cool like that.

'Can I talk to you?'

'Sure,' I said.

She nodded me toward the Train.

I went in, bringing a lantern. I hadn't been in the Train in . . . how long? More than twenty-four hours, to be sure.

It was easy to remember that these had been the dressing rooms of the Greenway, before they became our sleeping quarters. They still looked pretty commercial,

DAY 12

no matter how homey Josie had tried to make them when she redecorated.

On the doors to the rooms were written the names of the kids who'd slept there.

'Max, Batiste, and Ulysses' read the door to my right in Josie's handwriting.

That made me feel sad and scared. I missed Josie. I missed all of them.

Astrid followed my gaze.

'Do you think they could be there yet?' Astrid asked me.

'Maybe. I sure as hell hope so.'

'Yeah, me too' Astrid said. She was looking down at her feet. She was still wearing the knit hat I'd given her after she'd had me cut her hair.

I smiled, remembering that moment – probably the only nice thing she and I had ever shared.

Suddenly Astrid looked up and the glow from the lantern lit up her face.

A gleam of gold glinted off her nose ring. The nose ring made her look cool, but also a little fierce, too.

I must have been staring at her, wondering what she would look like without it.

'I'm not going to sleep with you,' she said.

And I nearly swallowed my heart.

'Wh-what?' I stammered.

'I just want you to know. I figured you might think that because you stayed, I would, like, sleep with you. And I'm not going to.'

Then she turned and walked out of the Train.

I just stood there like an idiot, with my mouth on the floor, for at least ten minutes.

Then I got angry.

I caught up with her in the Kitchen. She was starting to go through the shelves, pulling out food we didn't need to heat up to be able to eat.

'Astrid, I never expected you to sleep with me! I never said anything about that. I would never think or expect something like that!'

'Fine,' she said. 'Good. Then we're straight.'

'I stayed because you were right. It was too dangerous for the other kids, to have us with them. And I stayed because you told me you're pregnant. And staying was the decent thing to do.'

'And I'm grateful,' she said, overarticulating her words, like she thought I was an idiot. 'But I'm not going to sleep with you just because I'm grateful.'

'I can't believe you're saying this,' I stammered. 'Do you think I'm some kind of animal?'

'I just wanted to get the facts straight,' she said, turning her back on me.

'Well, they're straight.'

'Good,' she said, returning to her sorting. 'I'm glad to hear that.'

I was furious. She was acting so cold and so . . .

I don't know. I turned and walked away.

DAY 12

Had I been nursing a dream we'd get together and fall in love, and one day, one day far in the future, maybe we'd have sex?

Yes. Dur. Of course I had. That's what you do when you have a horrible crush on someone.

Now it felt like she was calling it out. Just saying it right in the open. It wasn't kind and it wasn't fair.

I stormed away into the dark, messy aisles of our stupid, commercial refuge.

I needed a project.

4 ALEX

NIKO HAD BLISTERS COMING up all over his face. I guess the mask got pushed to the side during the fight with Josie.

I guess the blisters were in his mouth, too. Or his lungs.

Niko rooted around in the plastic storage tub of medicines and found a bottle of Children's Benadryl.

He broke the seal and chugged straight from the bottle.

'Can't drive,' he gasped. 'We'll rest. Ten minutes.'

He slumped in a seat and bowed his head, trying to breathe.

'Can we take our masks off?' Max asked.

'NO!' Sahalia and I both shouted at once.

'Only people who are type B can take their masks off,' Sahalia said.

'Who's that again?' asked Batiste.

'You and me and Alex,' Sahalia said, rolling her eyes.

I shrugged and took off my mask.

53-42 MILES

The air had a taste to it. A stingy taste.

But it was much easier to talk, easier to see, and also, in a way, easier to think because you didn't have to listen to your scary breathing right in your ears.

Batiste took his off sheepishly. Max and Ulysses muttered together about fairness.

'What do we do now?' Sahalia asked, her hands on her hips.

'I guess we just wait,' I said. 'Niko, you tell us when you can drive, okay?'

Niko's head was lolled back on the seat.

I went up to him and put my head on his shoulder.

'Niko? Niko!' I called.

And then I heard him snore.

'Oh, this is perfect!' Sahalia complained.

'Niko, we need to get going,' I said. 'Niko, wake up.'

Niko sat up and looked around, as if confused.

'Just let me sleep for a few minutes,' he muttered. 'I'm so tired.'

He hadn't slept in . . . well, in more than 24 hours, maybe as long as 36 hours. But still.

It was murder, waiting. We gave him 10 good minutes.

'Okay, Niko. Time to get up!' I shook him.

'I can drive,' Sahalia said.

'What? No, you can't!'

'My stepdad lets me drive all the time,' she insisted.

'That's a horrible idea. This is a bus. A big school bus.'

'*I can drive*,' Sahalia shouted.

'Let her drive,' mumbled Niko. And he fell back asleep.

* * *

Okay, well, Sahalia wasn't terrible at driving the bus. She went maybe a little faster than Niko, but I didn't care. Josie was sedated. The kids were terrified and Niko had drugged himself into oblivion with Benadryl – the faster we got to DIA the better.

We were passing a burned-up commuter bus when a masked figure lurched out in front of us.

Sahalia braked but she hit the guy. His head cracked on the side of the bus and then he was gone.

Sahalia wrenched the steering wheel too far to the right and suddenly we were lurching down the embankment.

The terrain near the highway was fairly sparse – not a lot of trees or vegetation. Rolling hills with some dead underbrush. The underbrush slowed the roll of the bus, I think.

It didn't crash, just slowed to a stop. Sahalia was basically standing on the brake, too.

The kids were crying.

Niko staggered up from where he'd been sitting.

'What happened?' he shouted.

'Sahalia drove the bus off the road,' I said. Then, when she gave me a look that would kill, I added, 'By accident.'

'Okay,' he said. He seemed pretty wobbly on his feet.

He coughed and more blood appeared on the inside of his mask.

He looked out at the area. It seemed pretty deserted.

'I think we're safe enough!'

I nodded. I knew what he meant.

Niko meant we were safe enough to sleep for a while.

'We're hungry,' Max complained to me.

53-42 MILES

They had said they were hungry before, but that was when we thought we were going to be in Denver in a few hours. Now it looked like we were staying put for the night.

'So eat,' I told him. 'The food's over there.'

I pointed out an open bin filled with food.

Why did the kids need my help to rip open a bag of trail mix?

'You guys have to take care of yourselves! I am not in charge of you,' I said.

He had started crying.

I sighed and put my hand out to Max.

'Sorry,' I said.

I thought he would shake my hand, but instead he fell toward me and then I realized: He was giving me a hug.

Hard to tell, with all the layers. But I think it made him feel better.

Then he said, 'We're so hungry.'

'For God's sake, Max, if you're hungry, eat!' I said.

'But how?' he asked.

'What do you mean, how? Open your mouth, put the food in, and chew!'

He tapped on the plastic eye panel of his face mask.

'How do we get the food in?'

I felt stupid. I hadn't thought of that.

I went back to try to help them. They ended up just lifting the edges of their masks and jamming the food in.

I saw Max's skin get red and blisters came up, so after he'd had the chance to shove a couple mouthfuls of trail mix in, I took it away from them.

They lay down to sleep.

I tried to stay up and keep watch, but I was as tired as everyone else.

I do not know why no one came poking around the bus.

Maybe it was because the bus looked so crappy from the outside.

It was covered with splotches made by the paste that Robbie had the little kids use to seal any cracks or dings. The windows were boarded up.

It probably looked like it had died a long time ago.

53–42 MILES

5 DEAN

I DECIDED TO MAKE THE Train and the Living Room into more of a contained unit – a little home within the bigger store. That way we could light it and heat it when needed, and make it cheerful and less scary for the little kids.

It was a good big project. I needed a big project to distract me from what had happened between me and Astrid.

First I took my flashlight and went to the Toy Department. I had noticed that the row dividers there, unlike most of the other ones, appeared to be on wheels. They were locked down, of course, but they could be moved.

I unlocked one from the aisle that held the board games. The divider had shelves (as opposed to hooks).

That was great, I realized – we could use the shelves for supplies.

I got down and figured out how to unlock the wheels. Then I pushed it back to the Train.

It was hard work. The row divider was tall (maybe seven feet tall?) and heavy and unwieldy. It didn't roll well, of course, so I had to push it at an angle, like a bad shopping cart.

I was sweating and my chest was heaving by the time I got it to the Living Room.

It was long and would make up one wall of the three-sided room I was planning to set around the Living Room.

Astrid and the kids were over in the Kitchen. Probably having lunch.

I didn't want to feel left out, but of course I did.

I focused on my plan to reconfigure our living arrangements.

We would end up with the carpeted living space outside the berths, where our 'kitchen' and main supplies would be. And then we'd have the Train, with our beds, right there. We would only need to go out to go to the Dump and get more supplies.

There was probably a part of my mind that was aware that I was moving forward as if we would be staying in the Greenway for a long, long time, but all I could think of in the moment was that I wanted to show Astrid that I had good ideas and that I was smart and independent and I could move really heavy things.

That's the truth.

DAY 12

By the time I wrangled the second divider to the Living Room, Astrid and the kids were back from the Kitchen. Astrid and I ignored each other.

She wordlessly handed me a peanut butter and jelly sandwich and I wordlessly ate it and got back to work.

PB&Js are delicious, but I guess that's common knowledge.

The kids were trying to play a board game under the Christmas tree lights. Caroline was lying on her side as she played. She looked wiped out.

'Dean, come play Monopoly with us,' Chloe commanded. 'Caroline and Henry just aren't getting it.'

'No!' I snapped.

The three kids' heads popped up and Astrid looked at me, a question in her eyes.

I guess in the Greenway, a sharp tone from any of us O types required immediate risk assessment.

'I'm fine,' I said. 'Forget it.'

I walked away.

Let them stare.

Monopoly belonged to me and Alex. It was our game and they would never understand. There were strategies and traditions and they would never get all its complexities.

I didn't want them to play it.

I strode to the Toy Department for another divider, thinking that I would never play Monopoly with anyone besides Alex ever. Ever, ever, ever, ever.

It was possible I was behaving somewhat like a child.

And it was probably for the best that I was working on a big project that required me to move heavy objects.

Picking out a third divider gave me some trouble. I got one halfway there, but a wheel got stuck and wouldn't roll, so I had to go back for another.

As I was on my belly in the Toy Department, working on unlocking the latches on a new divider, I heard Astrid's quiet footsteps come up behind me.

'Dean,' she said. 'I'm sorry if I was . . . too mean or something before.'

She didn't sound sorry, she sounded worried.

Looking up at her, from the floor, I could see her belly under the bottom edge of her thermal top.

There was that rise. The little bump.

It suddenly kind of hit me that she was *pregnant*. That maybe I should remember that and give her a break if she acted . . . hormoney.

'Can you please just come?' she said.

I sat up and looked at Astrid.

She was sort of chewing on her lip.

'Caroline fell asleep and when I went to move her . . . She's hot. Really hot.'

'It's not my fault,' Chloe noted as I approached. She was loitering outside the 'bedroom' she and the twins shared. 'I'm just saying, just because of the whole rat thing, not everything is my fault.'

Two crib mattresses took up the entire floor space of their bedroom.

DAY 12

They had covered the mirror with crayon drawings of houses, trees, families – all the normal subjects of little kid drawings. The circumstances of our living situation made them all more poignant, of course.

The one that really killed me was a drawing by Henry with three people. I say people, but they were basically just smiling, potato-shaped ovals with lines for arms and legs. Long, spider-legged fingers sprouted from the ends of the arms and overlapped – the three figures were holding hands. The one on the left had a small red blob on its head. The one on the right had long red scribbles for hair, and the one in the centre had brown skin and two black knots on the top of her head.

Josie. It was a picture of Josie and the twins.

God, I wished Josie was here.

Caroline looked pale and sweaty. She was lying on the mattress on the floor, the sheets and blankets twisted and messy.

Henry was lying next to Caroline. His face was pressed right up to hers.

'She's not contagious,' he said to me defensively. 'I can be here.'

'Of course you can be here,' I agreed.

I knelt on the mattress. The whole chamber stank. I saw some old clothes and maybe some used pull-ups shoved into corners. The twins were too afraid to get up in the night to go to the Dump, so they used pull-ups. But never mind that.

'Hey, Caroline,' I said softly. 'How ya doing?'

She opened her eyes and looked at me. Her eyes were glassy and big.

'I'm good,' she said.

Tears leaked out of the corners of her eyes. She didn't wipe them away. They got on Henry, because his face was pressed right up to the side of hers. He didn't brush the tears away either.

'I'm going to take a look at your leg.'

I pulled at the covers twisted around her legs.

'Her leg's hot,' Henry said.

As I moved the sheets I saw that Henry had his foot pressed onto the bandage on Caroline's leg.

'What are you doing?' I asked him.

'I let my foot get cold, then I press it on her leg and it helps. Then I switch it when my foot gets hot again. It's helping! Right, Caro? It's helping.'

Caroline nodded weakly.

'We can do better than that,' I said. 'Henry, move out of the way for a moment, will you?'

'Okay,' he agreed reluctantly.

I carefully lifted Caroline's leg and pulled the Band-Aid off. She whimpered.

The wound was swollen, red around the edges and white in the centre. It was definitely infected.

A knot of dread hit my stomach like a punch. Why hadn't I treated her with antibiotics straightaway? What was wrong with me?

Silently I railed against my own stupidity. I had to start thinking like a leader.

DAY 12

'I'm fine,' she said, looking scared.

'Yup,' I said. 'You're just fine. But you know what, I'm going to give you a little bit of medicine. Just to make you feel even better.'

'Okay,' she answered.

I stood up and Henry settled back into his place.

'Don't . . . don't put your foot on her anymore, Henry. I'll get you something cool you can put on it for her.'

Something sterile, for God's sake.

Astrid followed me to the Pharmacy.

'It's bad, isn't it?' she asked me.

'It's bad. But we have a whole pharmacy here. We can fix it.'

'Luna won't come out either,' Astrid said. 'I put a can of dog food out for her and she won't touch it.'

The Pharmacy was still a mess, but after a while, I found what I was looking for – a Super-Z pack.

'What's that?' Astrid asked.

'Antibiotics.'

'How do you know they're the right ones?'

'I cut my leg on a garden stake last summer. Got really red and ugly. This is what the doctor gave me.'

'What about the dosage, though?' She was twisting her hands together, wringing them.

'Astrid, I don't know,' I said. 'This is our best option.'

'It had to be said, you know,' she asserted, changing the subject.

'That's just the thing,' I replied. 'It didn't. I would never have—'

She crossed her arms and edged away from me.

I took a breath and started again.

'Let's just face it. We hardly even know each other,' I said. 'So anything that you might have thought about me and anything that I might have thought about you – let's just put it all aside and start from scratch. Because look, maybe if we do that, we could actually get to be friends.'

I was probably getting a little carried away, but she was listening to me, so I went with it.

'Real friends, who can depend on each other. God knows we need to be able to do that. What do you think?' I asked.

'Yeah,' Astrid agreed. 'That's a good idea.'

It *was* a good idea.

And it *would* have been a good idea for me to somehow be able to actually do it and not be in love with her as we began again.

But she held out her hand for me to shake it.

And all right, maybe she didn't feel a thing, but when I took her hand in mine a jolt shot up my arm and struck me in the centre of my chest.

I couldn't pretend it away – I had it bad for Astrid Heyman.

But maybe I could do a better job of hiding it.

Caroline couldn't swallow pills.

She would put it in her mouth and take a sip of

DAY 12

Gatorade, but then she'd sputter and spit the pill (and the Gatorade) into her hand. It made a huge mess in their bedroom.

'I know what to do,' Chloe offered. 'You gotta take it in jelly. That's what my nana always did!'

And she was off in a chubby flash, hurrying to the decimated Food aisles.

She was right, though. Mashed up in a teaspoon of jelly, Caroline could take the antibiotics. It took us four teaspoons of jelly to get the two capsules down.

Astrid and I moved her out into the Living Room and set her on the couch.

I told the other two they had to do a thorough wipe-down with baby wipes and change clothes. They had dirty faces and smelled not good.

There was the prerequisite whining and complaining from Chloe.

'While you kids get clean, Astrid and I are going to clean out the Train,' I told them. 'We're making a new house and everything has to be nice in the new house.'

'A new House,' Caroline repeated sleepily.

We spent the next couple hours doing a complete overhaul of the Train. Astrid helped me move the last divider into place.

It really did feel like a House with a capital H – there was a kitchen area with shelves with food on them and a cook stove. There was a living room area with the futon couches and the bookshelf and then there was the Train, with our bedrooms inside it.

Chloe and Henry were delighted with the new House. They helped Astrid stock the shelves facing in with nonperishable food; select toys, books and games; and medical supplies.

'Dean!' Chloe shouted, coming back, arms laden with bags of cookies. 'Our House is a secret!'

Caroline stirred in her sleep and Astrid shushed Chloe.

'She's right,' Henry added. 'It really looks like a secret. Can we make it look like a better secret?'

'Can we, like, disguise it?' Chloe asked.

'What do you mean?' I said.

They dragged me through the gap to look.

It did look like 'a secret.' In the dark store, if you didn't know where to look, you might not have known there was a House there at all. The dividers made it look like a continuation of the Store's walls. Sort of. At least in the dark, it looked that way.

'See where the shelves are empty?' Chloe pointed. 'If we fill them up it will look more regular.'

'Okay.' I shrugged.

'Then we just have to figure out how to build a wall up there.' Henry pointed up.

Over the top of the dividers, light came from the House. He wanted to build a wall so the light wouldn't come through.

'That would be pretty impossible,' I told him.

'We could use blocks! We could build it with Legos!' he chirped.

DAY 12

'We do have plenty of Legos,' I conceded. 'Okay.'

It would be good for them to have something to do. But I was kind of surprised to see him so happy.

'Hey, Henry, aren't you worried about Caroline?' I asked.

He shrugged, his freckled face completely at ease.

'She's getting better now,' he told me.

'Really, how do you know?'

'I can just feel,' he said simply.

'Come on, Henry, let's get stuff to fill the shelves,' Chloe entreated.

The two clicked on their headlamps and skipped off into the darkness.

I went back in through the gap.

'Hey,' I said to Astrid, smiling, 'Henry says Caroline's getting better.'

I put my hand to the sleeping girl's forehead. It seemed slightly cooler.

'Really?' Astrid asked. She bent over and felt Caroline's head. 'Yeah, I think he's right. Wow, those pills work fast!' And she smiled that beaming smile that always kills me. In the warm light from our LED lamps, she looked even more pretty.

'That's a big relief,' I said, trying to play it cool.

'I'm worried about Luna, though.'

'I've been thinking about Luna,' I said. 'I have an idea.'

I went over to one of the coolers we had set up.

There was some hamburger thawing in there.

I took out a pack and sat on the ground near the couch.

'Can dogs eat raw hamburger?' Astrid asked.

'Oh yeah,' I answered. 'They love it. My uncle Dave has like four black Labs. Most beautiful dogs I've ever seen. He feeds them all a raw diet. He makes them this casserole out of hamburger and grated vegetables and flaxseed oil.'

'Jeez, that sounds . . . horrible.'

'You should never be a dog, then,' I told her.

'Duly noted.' She laughed.

I loved hearing her laugh.

Okay, I could be her friend and I could make her laugh. Maybe that could be enough.

'Hey, Luna girl,' I called softly. I stretched out my arm, offering the meat to Luna's shaking form. 'Mmmm . . . hamburger. Mmmmm . . . it's so yummy.'

I heard a soft whine.

'Come on out here, girl,' I called.

And slowly, Luna edged out toward the meat.

Given my luck, it would not have surprised me if she had rabies from the rat and attacked me.

But, no, she was just hurt and tired.

She took the meat from my fingers and licked them. She had a sort of grateful look in her eyes and her tail wagged twice.

I fed her the rest of the patty and then she took some water.

DAY 12

She tried to go back under the couch but I scooped her gently into my arms.

'Can you hand me the Bactine and the Neosporin?' I asked Astrid.

She handed them to me silently.

'That's a girl,' I said to the dog. 'We'll get these cuts healed up now. Good girl.'

I put some more ointment on the worst of the scratches. They looked red – more red than Caroline's bite wounds, but I really didn't know what else to do.

I had sat on the floor for so long, my knees were creaky when I stood up.

I turned and faced Astrid.

She was just looking at me with this weird look on her face.

'You're a good guy,' she said. Her voice sounded kind of hollow.

'Yeah,' I answered.

She laughed. It was a dry, self-deprecating chuckle.

'My mom said that when she met my dad she literally heard, like, a bell ringing and she had the thought, "This is a good guy." Like, she had this sudden recognition.'

I nodded.

'It didn't stop her from dating a long string of a-holes, I tell you that.'

'Your parents got divorced?'

'My parents never even married. She couldn't take it, how nice he was.'

'Oh,' I said. The conversation didn't seem like it was

going my way.

'Why do you think Jake left?' she asked, suddenly changing the subject.

'Uh. I think he wanted to help Brayden. He felt bad that when Brayden got shot, he couldn't do more . . .'

'Yeah, I know why he left the store *originally*. He was being a big hero. Going out scouting. Going on a big, stupid mission.'

There was bitterness in her voice. She was talking about Jake with her usual toughness, but I could almost hear how hurt Astrid was under the sarcasm.

'But after he showed us on the video walkie-talkie thing that the hospital was closed, why didn't he come back?'

'I don't know,' I told her.

'I'll tell you why,' she said. 'Because he only ever thinks about himself. That's the kind of guy I pick.'

Tears started to trickle down her cheeks.

'He doesn't even know,' she spat. 'About the baby. Ugh! What's wrong with me? I'm just totally falling apart!'

She wiped the tears roughly with the back of her hand.

'And where are the other guys? Have they made it? Shouldn't they be in Denver by now? Why hasn't anyone come back for us?'

She sank down to sit on the futon. She was really crying now. I didn't know what to do, so I sat down, too, and hugged her. It seemed like the right thing to do. It seemed like she needed someone to hold her.

I don't think I was taking advantage.

DAY 12

Her soft body felt so warm in my arms.

I hoped I wasn't taking advantage.

'Astrid, I know. It's horrible. It's all horrible.'

Lame.

She sobbed and I held her closer.

'I feel like I'm going crazy.' She wept into my shirt.

'Listen, Astrid, if I were you, I'd feel the same way,' I told her. 'We've lost everything and we don't know what's going to happen to us and, if all that wasn't enough, you're pregnant. You're pregnant, Astrid. You have to give yourself a break. You really do.'

She looked up at me. Wet lashes, reddish nose. Her beautiful face just inches away from mine.

She reached up and with her fingertips she straightened my glasses.

I could feel her breath on my lips.

She looked into my eyes.

And then Chloe and Henry came in, arms full of Lego bins stacked three high.

'What's wrong, Astrid?' Henry said. 'Are you sad? Don't cry.'

He came over to us, pushed me aside, and wriggled onto her lap, wrapping his skinny, freckled arms around her neck.

'Yeah,' Chloe added. 'Quit crying.' She emptied a Lego bin onto the floor. 'We've got a Lego wall to do and it's not going to build itself.'

6 ALEX

MORNINGS OUTSIDE GO LIKE This: You are in the dark and it looks like night. Like a very dark night with no moon at all. But this part of your brain is on a timer, waiting for the sky to get light at the edge. That kind of muddy grey sky, before it even gets light. You're just waiting for that and waiting for that and it never comes.

By my watch, I knew it was 6:07 a.m.

But it was dark, dark, dark.

Morning was never coming, it seemed.

Niko was feeling better, thank God.

He got everyone up, except for Josie. She was still out cold.

Brayden seemed the same as before. Still not really conscious but not dead either. Sahalia kept squeezing a little bit of Gatorade into his mouth every once in a while.

42-27 MILES

Sahalia, Batiste, and I had to get out and push to get the bus out of the ravine.

The ground was very muddy, with slime on it from the decaying leaves and grasses.

Niko was mad that Sahalia, Batiste, and I have our masks off, but really, it's impossible to hear what anyone says with them on. At least when we talked to him or to the little kids, one side of the conversation could be understood.

And of course, we weren't the best choice to push the bus, but even Niko had to agree that we were the right ones, since we're all type B.

We rocked and rocked the bus. The wheels had a thin layer of that fuzzy white mould on them, but it didn't seem to matter. Eventually the bus rolled forward and got traction on some underbrush.

We got back on.

'Ugh,' Sahalia said, wiping some muck off the front of her top layer, a men's Windbreaker, probably 5 sizes too big. 'It reeks out there.'

'I think it's decayed vegetation,' I told her.

'Whatever, geek,' she said as she plopped herself down next to Brayden.

If we two were the two last people on earth – not, by the way, as statistically implausible as it was a month ago – she would still be rude to me and I would still pretend that it didn't bother me.

Niko drove. We were driving along the bottom of the ditch, parallel to the highway. The hill we had slid down was not too high. I would estimate 15–20 feet.

I was thinking about Dean. I knew he'd be worried. We should have made it to DIA by now. We should have sent a rescue party by now.

Soon Niko pointed to a big road sign.

We had to pick whether to take I-25 to I-225 or to go right and take the tollway.

'The tollway is more direct,' I said. 'But it will probably be more used, because other people would also choose the most direct route. On the other hand, I-225 runs through more densely populated areas, I think, because it gets closer to Denver.'

Niko thought for a minute and then, without saying anything, he took the tollway.

Oh, Dean.

It's so bad.

It's so bad what happened.

We took the toll road and we were making good time. We'd reached Parker, so that means we had gone about halfway to DIA.

I saw something standing in the road.

The light from the headlights bounced off it and it was a gleaming shape. Like a ghost.

'There!' I said. 'Something white.'

I wiped at the Plexiglas windshield and squinted out. I saw it was a girl.

She was wearing a white coat, somehow it was not too dirty, and her face was uncovered.

'Stop! It's a girl,' I shouted.

She had long blonde hair. That white-blonde like Max has.

She held up her hands for us to stop. Her hands were bare.

Niko slowed but didn't stop.

He honked the horn.

'Niko, you have to stop!'

'No!' he shouted. 'Too risky.'

The girl opened her mouth and I could see she was screaming for us to stop, though I couldn't hear her.

'Stop!' Sahalia shouted.

The little kids joined in, too.

Niko slammed on the brakes. 'I don't like it,' I heard him say.

I opened the door mechanism. 'Get in!' I shouted to the girl.

Then I saw them coming.

The darkness started moving, is what it looked like. And then shapes came out of it and I saw they were boys. Teenage boys in camouflage. Their faces had been painted, or maybe they'd used mud.

Three of them rushed at me and I pulled the door shut. They banged on it.

Niko tried to back up, but they'd gotten something behind the bus. I didn't know what. But he kept trying to reverse and crashing into something over and over. (It was 2 motorcycles.)

Two of them rolled a dead motorcycle in front of the bus.

We were trapped.

One of them, I guess the leader, came in front of the bus and tapped the butt of a rifle against the Plexiglas.

He was wearing a scarf tied around his mouth and a black beret on his head. His eyes were rimmed with red and they looked wild.

'Who are they?' Sahalia screamed.

'Cadets!' Niko answered. 'Air Force cadets!'

'He's O. He's O!' I shouted.

Niko laid on the horn.

'Get out of the way!' Niko shouted and immediately started coughing.

'Out of the way!' I yelled.

'Screw you!' the leader shouted. 'We want the bus!'

'Tell them they can come with us,' Niko said to me. He couldn't yell loud enough for them to hear, through the mask.

'You guys can come!' I shouted. 'We're going to the airport.'

'If they throw down their guns,' Niko added.

'If you throw down your guns!'

The leader jammed the butt of his rifle into the glass. 'They're *killing* people at DIA! Don't you idiots know that?' he shouted. 'They're sorting them into groups and *killing* people who saw it go down. They don't want any witnesses!'

I looked at Niko.

Sahalia was behind us.

'He's crazy,' she said. 'He's paranoid.'

Three other cadets had come to stand around their leader.

'*He* might be crazy,' I pointed out. 'But what about the rest of them?'

They were all wearing camouflage fatigues. None of them wore gas masks. I guess the rest of them were either type AB or B.

'Where's the girl?' I wondered aloud.

Then there was a bang and the little kids were screaming.

I turned to see a cadet climbing in one of the back windows. He'd hacked it down with some kind of hatchet.

One of them started kicking in the door.

Niko got up and grabbed his backpack, which I know had the gun in it.

But before he could get the gun out, the cadet got the door open and they were inside.

'Jesus!' the leader shouted. 'This bus is stocked!'

He let out a crazy, happy whoop and picked Sahalia up and kissed her on the mouth. She squirmed away as Niko shouted. 'Get your hands off her!'

The leader smacked Niko across the face.

Niko's mask came off a little bit and the guy grabbed it, holding it off his face.

'Stop it!' I screamed. 'He'll die!'

I kicked him and he let the mask go and turned on me.

He grabbed me by my jacket.

'I tell you what, you tell me everything I want to know and I'll let your driver keep his gas mask. How's that?'

Niko was gasping through the air mask. Sahalia was on the floor in the aisle. She started pulling Josie out of the aisle, away from us.

The other cadets were coming up the steps now. They were high-fiving one another, happy about their conquest.

'First off, what's with him?' the leader asked, nodding at Josie.

'Him?' I stalled. My mind hiccupped – he thought Josie was a boy – okay, I would go with that. 'He's type O and we had to—'

'And that guy?' he cut me off, nodding toward Brayden.

'Brayden? He got shot,' I said. 'We're taking him to the airport to find a doctor.'

'Jesus Christ!' he yelled and I saw his cadets jump. 'Didn't you hear what I said? They're *killing* people at the airport. They're out to get us all. Brayden here is dead. He's as good as dead.'

Was that true? I didn't think so. This guy was clearly crazy.

Sahalia started to sob. I do not know why she did that. It drew the leader's notice.

'Aw, did you have a little something for Brayden? Don't cry, baby. Payton will watch out for you.'

He put his hand down and touched her on her face.

'I'll take good care of you, honey. You can be my special girl.'

Niko tried to get forward so he could, I don't know, jump on the guy, but the cadets near the door stopped him.

'How'd your bus not get skunked?' Payton demanded.

'Skunked?'

He rolled his eyes.

'The white fuzz. It grows on rubber. Eats the tyres. Where'd you get the bus?'

'We were locked inside a store with the bus,' I said. 'We sealed in the air, so it wasn't exposed—'

'So you left a big sealed-in store, filled with food and water, to try to get Brayden here to Denver?'

'Yeah.' I shrugged.

'And how long you been on the road?'

'What do you mean?'

'How many hours you been on the *road*? After twenty-four hours, tyres start to skunk.'

'We left the store around 10 a.m. yesterday—'

'Sweet! They still got some play left in 'em. Last question . . .' he said, turning back to me. 'Where's the store?'

I caught Niko's eye and he shook his head just a bit.

'The King Soopers,' I lied.

'Which one?'

'In Castle Rock.'

'Which. Effin'. One?'

'The one . . . the one . . .'

'You're a LIAR!' he shouted.

Then he ripped me across the face. I don't think it would have cut me if he hadn't been wearing a ring.

It felt like fire across my face and then there was blood on my gloves and running down my neck.

Batiste shouted it out: 'We came from the Greenway in Monument,' he yelled. 'The Greenway in Monument, Colorado.'

Payton laughed. 'Now *that* I believe!' He smiled at Batiste. 'All right, boys, we're going to Monument!'

'Brayden will die!' Sahalia screamed. 'He's going to die if we don't get to Denver!'

Payton pulled her to him.

'You give me a kiss and I'll get him there, honey.'

Her eyes got really big and scared. She leaned up on her tiptoes and kissed his filthy cheek.

I was afraid he'd grab her and kiss her hard. Or worse.

Instead he put his hand up to his cheek.

'Mmmmmm, sweetness,' Payton said. 'You're nothing but a little thing, aren't you?' He put his finger under her chin and made her look up at him.

Sahalia is some kind of magnet for jerks, I think.

'For you, little girl, I'm gonna save Brayden! Doolies!' Payton shouted. 'We have to save this boy.'

'Sir, yes, sir!' the cadets shouted.

'We're gonna take him to Denver.'

Then he grabbed me by the jacket and shoved me into the aisle.

'Now, get out. You all get out. We're going to take Brayden to Denver now.'

'What?' The little kids were crying.

'GET OUT!' Payton shouted. He pushed Sahalia toward the door. 'Even you, my little sweetmeat. You have to go, too, so Daddy Payton can get the job done.'

It happened so fast. He was kicking us out of the bus and we didn't have a moment to think or anything.

'Hey, we have to get Brayden to Denver and we can't achieve our mission with a bunch of pukey, crying sissies loading us down!'

I didn't even have my backpack but I looked back and saw Max grabbing all the backpacks he could find. Ulysses started grabbing stuff, too.

Payton reached over and snatched the backpacks away from Max.

Max let out a cry and the leader picked him up and threw him down the aisle, toward the door.

'This stuff is ours now! You get me? All this bus and everything on it is ours! So you better get off if you don't want to be ours, too!'

A short, greasy-looking cadet grabbed the water bottles away from Ulysses and kicked him down the stairs.

Sahalia was trying to get back to Brayden now and one of the cadets was holding her back. He sort of wrestled her out the door and down the steps.

'Brayden! Brayden!' she sobbed.

Niko was still in the driver's seat. It seemed like he didn't know which way to go or what to do.

'Hey, driver boy,' Payton called to Niko, nudging Josie's hip with his boot. 'You'd better come and get this comatose kid if you want him!'

I wonder whether Payton would have let Niko take Josie if he'd known she was a girl. But with all the layers, who could tell?

Niko got up and went down the aisle toward Josie.

Payton leaned down and sniffed Brayden. 'Ooof, man, Brayden smells ripe. We'd better get to Denver right away to get him to a hospital!'

Niko picked up Josie and half carried, half dragged her off the bus.

I noticed he had his backpack on.

I noticed it because I was right behind him.

'Brayden!' Sahalia was screaming from outside. 'I love you!'

That made the cadets laugh.

'*I love you, Brayden*,' they mimicked.

'Come on, doolies! We gotta get this jack-up to Denver!' Payton yelled.

A cadet dragged a crushed motorcycle out from behind the bus.

'To Denver!' They were cheering. 'To Denver!' But the way they said it, mocking and overexcited, you could tell they weren't really going to Denver.

'You can't just take our bus!' Batiste shrieked at two of the cadets.

'Oh yeah?' said a really tall, gangly cadet. He pointed his gun at Batiste. 'Just watch.'

Now they were all on board and we were all off, besides Brayden.

The girl in the white coat slipped around the corner of the bus. She looked like she was afraid. She stepped up onto the first step of the bus.

66

'Hey!' I called to her. She looked at me, her big blue eyes open round and wide.

'You don't have to go with them. You can come with us,' I said. I thought maybe she was like their captive. Or their slave or something.

She took a long look and then she stuck her middle finger up at me.

42-27 MILES

7 DEAN

I SLEPT HARD AND, HALLELUJAH, I slept until I woke up of my own accord. Yes, I got to sleep in.

What woke me up was just the growl of my own stomach.

I went out into the Living Room and found the three kids building Lego walls while Astrid read on the couch. Breakfast had been eaten (cereal with soy milk, by the looks of it). Caroline was still in her PJs but looked better. Luna was even up and about.

Seeing me, Luna rose and came over to give my hand a hopeful sniff.

'Good morning,' Astrid said. 'I made you coffee.'

'Dean, when will they be here?' Chloe complained. 'I'm sick of waiting, already. All we do is wait and wait and wait—'

She was interrupted by a bang.

I turned to Astrid.

'What on earth?' she said blankly.

BANG. BANG.

It was coming from the front gate.

'Chloe, you stay here and take care of Caroline and Henry,' I ordered. She closed her mouth with a snap.

I grabbed a headlamp and Astrid took a flashlight, and together, we ran toward the front gate, winding our way through the dark, cold store.

Luna ran beside us, barking her head off.

BANG. BANG.

Someone was shooting at the gate.

'Stand back,' I told Astrid, throwing my arm out to block her. She stopped, close behind me, her body pressed against mine, and even in that moment of tension and fear, I was aware of her body.

We moved around to the side, out of the way of the gate.

'What do you want?' I yelled toward the closest bullet hole.

Luna was barking herself hoarse.

BANG. Another shot tore a tiny hole through the gate.

'Luna, shut up!' Astrid grabbed Luna's collar and held her back.

'Who are you and what do you want?' I hollered.

'Stop! Stop shooting,' I heard from outside. Had to strain to hear the voice.

DAY 13

Then there was a thud and a rattle on the gate, as if something or someone had been smashed against it.

'Hey, kid,' came the voice. 'It's me, Scott Fisher.'

'Why are you shooting our store? We already gave you food!' I yelled.

'That's just it, man. This guy here—'

And again came the thudding sound and a dull rattle from beyond the plywood.

'This guy here found me and he said I had to show him where I got the stuff, and if you don't give us more, he's going to kill me.'

I looked at Astrid, illuminated from below by her flashlight.

'Shoot,' I said.

'We have to help him,' Astrid pleaded.

'I know,' I said.

Scott Fisher gave a cry of pain.

'Okay,' I shouted. 'Okay!'

'He says you have to open the store!'

'We'll throw down food,' I shouted.

'He's going to kill me if you don't open the store!'

'Look, we can't open the store. But we'll throw down lots of food and water, okay?'

There was the sound of an argument, but we couldn't hear the words. I could hear the tone, though, and Scott's voice went higher and higher. Fighting? Begging?

Another rattle on the gate and now his voice was desperate.

'Watch out, kid! He's gonna—'

Another BANG. BANG. Then it was quiet and it seemed clear that Scott Fisher was dead.

'Gonna what?' Astrid said in a quiet, scared voice.

'I'm going to go look for weapons,' I told her. 'You stay here and hit the air horn if they try anything.'

Thank God we'd found those stupid headlamps.

I knew I looked like an idiot, but as I ran through the store, looking for weapons, I was glad I was wearing my flashlight on my head, and had my arms free.

If only Jake hadn't taken the one gun. We'd had two, from the outsiders.

And when he left, Niko had taken one. That was good. I wanted Niko to have one.

But Jake had taken the other gun and then walked out on us. I begrudged him that gun.

I thought of potato guns. I didn't know how to make them and I was pretty sure they took a long time to make.

There was some way to use aerosol cans to make blowtorches, but I didn't know how to do it.

What could I do? I guess I could go and get a bunch of knives from the Kitchen aisles and throw them at the intruders. So lame. I wanted to wring my own neck for being so lame.

'Dean?' came Chloe's voice. She must have heard me moving around in the aisles. 'What's happening out there?'

'It's nothing,' I shouted. 'You're doing a good job, Chloe. Just keep the twins there. Just wait for us. Everything's okay.'

DAY 13

'We're bored!'

'Just be bored, then,' I yelled. She was such a brat.

I raced toward Home Improvement.

Why had I spent time building us a room? I should have been making weapons.

I needed my brother, who could make anything out of anything. Or Niko, who just naturally thought in terms of survival.

I paced through the store, aisle after aisle.

Home Improvement seemed like the best option.

I came to the barbecues.

And the lighter fluid.

My best idea was to squirt it on them and light them on fire.

Stupid idea, I know, but I was in a panic.

Back at the gate, Astrid was poking putty into one of the holes in the gate.

'Are you okay?' I asked as I ran towards her.

I carried a case of lighter fluid and a couple of those long-neck fireplace lighters.

'They're gone,' she said quietly. 'At least for now.'

'Are you sure?'

'I haven't heard a sound.'

'Okay, okay, good,' I said.

'Were you going to barbecue them to death?' Astrid asked, her hands on her hips.

I was mad, for a second, then I saw her eyes twinkle in the glow from my headlamp.

And I started to laugh.

Her laughter joined me and it totally got away from us until I had tears coming down my face.

'Shoot,' I said. 'You're funny.'

'Sometimes,' Astrid answered. 'I got some wood putty. Want to help me plug up these bullet holes?'

'Sure,' I answered.

As we worked, I told her about an idea. 'I saw some chainsaws in Home Improvement. They're mostly kerosene, but there are a couple of battery-powered ones.'

I knew a little about chainsaws, because I'd helped my uncle clear some land down near Placerville during the summer. Uncle Dave had two chainsaws, one gas and one battery. The battery one was a lot less powerful than the gas one, but it cut scrub oak okay. I shuddered with the thought of what it would do as a weapon against a person.

'Can't you use the lighter fluid?' Astrid nodded toward my can of Kingsford.

I grabbed the bottle.

'No, it's not kerosene. It's . . . aliphatic petroleum solvent. Whatever that is.'

'Well, how are you going to charge the batteries?' she asked.

'Maybe a car battery?' I suggested.

'Yeah, that could work,' she said.

We were a good team. I was glad we had decided to work on being friends. She was holding up her end of the bargain and I was trying my best not to worship her.

DAY 13

'Where have you been? Do I have to do everything around here?' Chloe chided when we returned from hooking up the chainsaws. They were playing hospital, and Caroline, appropriately enough, was the patient.

'Bad guys were trying to get in,' Astrid told her.

'Bad guys?' Henry repeated.

He and Caroline looked up at us with an identical expression of fear in their two sets of eyes.

Every once in a while, taking care of the twins, I'd feel a sort of a lurch in my heart. They were so, erm, beautiful. I know that's a dorky word to use, but they were. Their smallness and warmth. Their wide-open smiles and abundance of freckles. It made my chest ache to think of how Mrs McKinley, if she were still alive, must be missing them. Whether it was in her honour or in her memory, I had to keep them safe.

'How bad?' Chloe asked.

'What?' I said.

'On a scale of one to ten, how bad were the bad guys?'

'I don't know,' I told her. 'Bad enough.'

'They couldn't get through the gate, though,' Astrid said. She ruffled Henry's hair. 'Too bad for them.'

Astrid had a pretty good approach with the kids. Josie would have withheld the truth, probably, and spun some story. But they seemed happier just knowing the facts: Bad guys had tried to get in and couldn't.

'Caroline, it's time for a sip of ginger ale,' Chloe directed.

Caroline sipped dutifully.

'Okay, now Henry's going to take your pulse,' Chloe said. Henry knelt by the futon and pressed his fingers somewhere in the vicinity of Caroline's elbow.

Henry and Caroline looked at each other with big, serious eyes.

'It's better!' he announced. 'One hundred nine and four eighty pressure.'

'Excellent,' Chloe nodded. 'Now the patient must eat more crackers.'

Henry fed his twin crackers a bite at a time, and Chloe looked on, content and the very model of efficiency.

'Dean, I had an idea,' Astrid said. 'I saw a brass fire pit in Home Improvement. I thought maybe I'd drag it over to the Kitchen. I don't want to light it in here, in case it gets too smoky, but I thought it might be kind of cheery to have a fire at night.'

'Yeah, sounds cool.' Exhaling, I ran a hand through my hair. So far, the morning had been pretty . . . intense. 'I'm going to eat some breakfast,' I told Astrid. 'And then I'm going to do a security check on the store.'

'Good idea,' she answered.

DAY 13

8 ALEX

NIKO HAD JOSIE IN his arms. Her head lolled back, bobbing loose. Sahalia was sobbing, clinging to Ulysses, who was also crying.

Me and the others were just standing there gaping. It was hard to grasp. Our bus had been taken and we were out in the dark.

'We have to get it back!' Sahalia shrieked. 'We have to attack them and get Brayden and kick them out!'

'Guys . . .' Max tried to butt in.

'How?' Niko said from behind his air mask. 'They have guns. There are five of them!'

'Guys!' Max yelled.

'We need to find somewhere safe until Josie wakes up. Then we'll figure out what to do.'

'They'll be far gone by then!' Sahalia protested.

'Guys!' Max shouted.

'What?' Niko yelled.

'I know where we can stay,' he said. Then he pointed over to a clump of dead trees. There was a military floodlight near there and in the glow you could make out a sign: 'Meadow Flowers Mobile Home Community.'

'What is it?' Batiste asked.

'It's a trailer park,' Max said loudly through his mask. 'My auntie Jean lives here.'

Niko was right; we had no choice. We couldn't catch up to the bus on foot. And if we somehow did, there was no way we could kick the cadets off it. We had to go and seek shelter.

It didn't keep Sahalia from crying and cursing the whole way.

Niko had to carry Josie. It did not look as easy as it looks in the movies. He had to stop and rest a lot and I was afraid his mask would come off.

The little kids were all clustered around me and I did not blame them; it was really scary.

Sometimes a fuse would blow at our house. I used to be scared to go into the basement to flip the switches. I was scared because the basement was so dark and there were things there in the darkness. You couldn't see them but you could feel them. Flattened boxes, Dad's old tools, the lawn mower – none of it scary with the lights on, but the thought of it all just lurking there made me scared. I would always be afraid that a murderer was hiding in the shadows, waiting to grab me, even though I knew that was totally illogical.

Walking down the road was like going into the dark basement, except that there really could be a murderer lurking in the shadows.

26 MILES

There was *likely* a murderer lurking in the shadows. It was statistically probable.

Maybe you are wondering if we didn't have flashlights. We did.

But Niko wouldn't let us use them. He said he was afraid we might call attention to ourselves.

(And call an O monster, I assume.)

So we had to see by the light from the military lights. Which was not very much.

We came to the Meadow Flowers entrance and walked through the trailer graveyard.

There was blood on one of the trailers and a lot of clothes out on the ground in between two others, all of them trampled into the mud. Purposely trampled, it seemed to me.

There were empty food cans and bottles from all kinds of drinks scattered everywhere.

Some of the trailers had furniture pulled halfway out the windows and doors. Like people had tried to take their easy chairs or mattresses and then given up.

A dead lady sat in a doorway in a house dress stuck to her body with blood.

Ulysses started to cry again and Max took his hand.

'We're almost there!' Max shouted through the mask, encouraging his friend.

There were lights on in a trailer we passed. I could hear an old man singing a country song my grandma used to sing called, 'Let's Give Them Something to Talk About,' by Bonnie Raitt.

We didn't knock.

Niko was having a hard time with Josie so I carried his backpack.

I should have thought of it before and offered but I was too scared, I guess.

Finally Max pointed to a baby-blue trailer on the fringe of the other trailers.

It was dark but there wasn't any blood and the windows weren't broken. I could see plastic over the windows inside. Another good sign.

Max stepped up on the step and knocked on the door.

'Auntie Jean!' he yelled. 'Auntie Jean?'

At first nothing.

And then he pounded on the door. 'Auntie Jean, it's me!'

Right at the corner of the window, the drape pulled away and a lady's hairline and eye and eyebrow appeared.

'Go away! I don't got nothing,' she yelled.

'Let us in!' he shouted.

'What do you want?' she yelled.

'It's me! It's me, Max! Max Skolnik! Jimmy's kid!'

The door opened.

I am not exaggerating, a cloud of cigarette smoke came out.

'Maxie?' she said, putting her face through the crack.

At that moment, I did not notice much about her beyond the fact that she had a gold tooth.

'It's me, Auntie Jean!' Max said.

And she threw open the door.

And we got inside somewhere safe, thank God.

This Jean lady cried for a real long time, hugging Max to her and sobbing into his white-blond hair until it looked kind of tan.

I am pretty sure she was drunk.

26 MILES

It was crowded in there, and smoky.

She told us that she'd been smoking nonstop because the smoke kills the compounds.

I didn't believe her but she was right! Cautiously, we took off our protective gear and everyone was okay.

This was very good information – prime information to have.

There were cigarettes everywhere, flowing out of ashtrays and jars and stacked up on paper plates and old issues of *Star News* magazine. There were also a bunch of smelly candles. Scented candles, I mean. And all the scents together, with the smoke, made it smell pretty dense in there. Flowers and vanilla and cranberry and dive-bar drunks.

I helped Niko and Jean get Josie up onto the bed in the back.

After we got Josie on the bed, Niko just slumped down to the floor and I saw he was crying.

'It's okay,' I said to him. 'There's nothing you could have done.'

'I blew it,' he said. 'We had a shot. I know we could have made it. But I blew it.'

He just turned his face to the side of the bed and cried.

I patted his back. I didn't know what to do. I'm not good when people cry. I do not know what to say and I just stand there flapping my arms like a stupid magpie.

I went into the front room where I saw that Sahalia was sitting in the banquette, facing away from the others and smoking a cigarette.

I shouldn't have been shocked, but I sort of was.

She rolled her eyes at me.

Max's auntie Jean was now helping the kids out of their layers. She was tugging a sweatshirt off Ulysses.

'Lord, you got some chunk on you, don't you, doll?' she asked Ulysses.

He smiled tentatively at her.

'Are you sure it's a good idea to take off their layers?' I asked her.

'The poison's in the cloth,' she answered me, her gold tooth glinting. 'Y'all got to take them off so I can get the air poison out.'

Batiste, Max, and Ulysses looked helpless. They were each standing in their underwear, fidgeting.

Sahalia, as you can only imagine, was having nothing to do with this. She took a long drag on her cigarette and shrugged at me.

Jean was wearing skinny jeans, high-heeled slippers, and one of those ladies' Christmas sweaters with the tall shoulders and the sparkly designs. It had a snowman on it with a pointy orange nose and fake gems for buttons on his snow stomach.

She took all the clothes she'd taken off Max, Batiste, and Ulysses and put them in a big garbage bag.

'Come on,' she said to me, snapping her fingers. 'Get down to your undies, pal, so I can do it all at once.'

'No way! Not in front of you two.' I indicated her and Sahalia.

'For Lord's sake, honey, I'm trying to keep us all safe here.'

She put her hands on her hips, a cigarette stuck in the corner of her mouth.

'I'm fine,' I insisted.

Jean went over to a coatrack on the wall and handed me a worn white robe that said 'Marriott' on it.

'Go on in the toilet and put this on and throw out your clothes,' she said.

'You can keep your drawers on.'

26 MILES

I should have left my long johns on. Sahalia snorted when I came back in the room wearing nothing but my tighty-whities under the robe. I wanted to punch her right in the cigarette.

Jean had pulled her straggly hair back and something was different from when we'd come in, just a few minutes ago. At first I couldn't place it. Then she took her cigarette out of her mouth and I realized what it was – there was now a lipstick stain on her cigarette.

But in all the butts on the table and near the door and all around the place, there wasn't lipstick.

She had put on lipstick at some point since we'd gotten there, maybe fifteen minutes before. She had put on lipstick for a bunch of kids.

Isn't that weird? I thought it was weird. And I do not know why I remembered it but I did.

'All right, now, I'll show you,' she said. 'This is how you clean your clothes nowadays.'

She took a huge drag off her cigarette and blew it into the bag with our clothes in it.

'You wanna help?' she said to Sahalia.

'I'll help!' Max offered.

'Are you drunk?' Jean said. 'Jimmy would kill me, I let his kid smoke.'

And then Jean started crying again, and Sahalia had to do all the smoke blowing by herself.

9 DEAN

FIRST I CHECKED ON the chainsaws. I detached the chainsaw battery from the car battery and inserted it into the chainsaw.

I pushed the button and VROOOOOM, the thing came to life. I shut it off quickly – didn't want to make Astrid worry or the kids come running.

But I was relieved. Now we had weapons of some kind. Not so good against bullets, but close up they'd be . . . horrific. Hopefully just holding one would be threat enough to make any intruders leave us be.

My next stop was the storeroom.

I wanted to make sure the hatch was properly locked and I also knew I should do something about the bodies.

I brought two chainsaws with me so I could bring them over to the House, when I was done in the

DAY 13

storeroom. I decided I should teach Astrid how to use one, just in case.

I was right – the bodies were beginning to smell.

I needed to seal them off somehow. My first idea was to put them in giant plastic bins. But none of the bins were big enough. Not by a long shot.

So then I turned to plastic sheeting, but we'd used all the plastic drop cloths when we sealed the gates.

I headed for the shower curtains. We had used some of those, but maybe not all.

And that's how Mr Appleton and Robbie came to be shrouded in floral nylon shower curtains.

Maybe it sounds funny. But it wasn't funny to me. It was a nightmare to roll them up in those curtains. Mr Appleton's body was heavy and rank and stiff, as if someone'd siphoned out his blood and replaced it with cement.

Robbie was grisly, with the blood, but the sheet we'd thrown on him stuck to his face, so at least I didn't have to look at him.

I got them wrapped up and I laid them side by side on the floor. The next step was to drag them over to the wall. Then I thought I might get some boxes or maybe decorative rocks or something and cover the bodies, so the kids wouldn't see them if they came into the storeroom.

And I needed to wipe down.

I smelled like something dead. Dead men, to be specific.

That's when I felt the hit.

There was a sound, like a big *THUNK*, but more than the sound, I felt the impact. The floor *shook*.

I grabbed a chainsaw and rushed back into the store.

'*Dean?*' I heard Astrid shout.

'I'm back here!" I yelled.

THUNK.

The impact came again. I was close to it.

I scanned around with my headlamp, trying to find what could be making that noise.

THUNK. And now a heavy chunking noise – the sound of cinder blocks caving in.

I scanned the wall, running from aisle to aisle. The sound was coming from the corner of the store near the storeroom, near the Dump.

'Someone's trying to break through!'

I saw Astrid's light come jagging toward me.

Then I saw the attack site. The cement bricks were caving in at the floor. Then they moved and we saw the reason.

Two metal prongs had crashed through the wall.

'It's a tractor or something,' I yelled.

The prongs retracted.

'They're trying to get in!' Astrid screamed.

Behind Astrid, Chloe and the twins appeared with Luna at their heels, barking her head off.

'Go back to the Train!' I yelled at them.

'You always say that!' Chloe shouted back.

More bricks crashed inside.

DAY 13

There was an opening maybe two feet across now, down at knee height.

'Get back!' I shouted.

I pulled the starter on my chainsaw and it roared to life.

'Dean,' Astrid yelled. '*Dean!* We need our masks!'

The tractor came back, puncturing higher this time. The hole was getting bigger. Blocks rolled inward, towards us.

Astrid pulled the kids away from the site.

'GET TO THE TRAIN! LOCK YOURSELVES IN, OR YOU'RE DEAD!' she hollered, dragging them back, back, back.

'Come on, Chloe!' Henry shouted and the twins hauled Chloe off toward the train.

Astrid took off toward the front gate. Going for masks, maybe.

I didn't care.

I could already feel my blood rising.

Who was trying to get in?

I would kill him.

Going to wreck our store?

I would kill him.

More cement blocks fell.

And I saw the front of the machine. It wasn't a tractor, it was a palette lifter.

My chainsaw roared and vibrated, shaking my arm.

I loved that chainsaw. It felt like a natural extension of my body.

And so I stepped over the rubble, on top of it, and ducked through, into the black world.

I was out and I was about to kill someone and I had never felt so alive or so full of blood or so bone-deep *fantastic* in all my life.

Luna raced out alongside me, barking her head off.

'Dean!' I heard Astrid call, her voice muffled. '*Dean*, careful!'

But I didn't need to be 'careful'. *No*. 'Kind' and 'considerate' were all in my mind. I was in my body now and the body had a strength that puny mind could never wield.

I pushed Dean, the whole personality, right out of my being.

I was the chainsaw now.

I vaulted over the prongs of the loader as it came forward again. The driver saw me coming but he was too slow. *Way* too slow.

He pulled out a pistol and aimed it at me, but I was moving so fast now.

Whirring, moving, slicing, I pulled him out of the loader and cut right through.

Neckarmtorso. Done.

Then through again. Shearing through torsobellyhip. Done.

Then my hands were wet and the chainsaw was lodged in the man's pelvis. The motor whined, growing louder and louder. It wanted more.

I pulled and pulled and meanwhile, I heard talking.

DAY 13

Voices.

A boy and a girl.

Something like, *Jake? Jake! I came back. You came back? I saw the guy attacking but I was too late. Help me. Dean's O!*

And I thought, Two to kill. Two to kill.

But my chainsaw was still stuck and whining. It was jammed with bone and had bit into the metal and I couldn't get it out.

I could kill them with my hands, though.

I ROARED and turned.

And then I was felled.

Jake.

He had hit me with something.

A cement block.

And I fell facedown on the ground. There was blood in my mouth and it tasted good.

Now I can kill Jake, I thought.

But then there was rope and he was tying me up.

I strained against the ropes as hard as I could, bucking and fighting. The rope cut into my wrists and ankles.

I bellowed in outrage, my face pressed onto the bloody asphalt.

He started dragging me back into the store, my arms and legs bound behind me.

Facedown on the pavement, I got dragged.

I would kill him. Jake was a dead man.

Then white-sneakered feet came close to my face.

And a gas mask came into view.

It was Astrid.

'Don't bite me!' she shouted through her mask.

'AAAAARRRRRRGH!' I shouted.

And she forced an air mask over my face and duct-taped it to my head.

Jake. Jake. Jake. My blood beat the name of the kid I would kill.

DAY 13

10 ALEX

I HAVE BEEN THINKING ABOUT it and I think it would have been better for all of us if Brayden had died on the bus.

Then Sahalia wouldn't be so mad at Niko, and Niko wouldn't be so mad at himself.

And Josie.

Well, when Josie wakes up, I think she will be very upset.

But if Brayden had just died, then we could all feel bad or sad or whatever, but get on with it.

Niko napped next to Josie for a while, then Jean made him wake up and give her his clothes to 'purify' them. He put on some men's clothes she had lying around.

Everyone was hungry so we had some trail mix and some cookies and some water. Jean took some and wolfed it down.

The speed at which she ate the cookies let me know that she

wasn't about to share any food with us. It let me know she didn't have much. Or any.

We went through Niko's backpack to take stock of what we had.

Of course, he had packed well, so there was a little of everything:

1. 2 40-ounce bottles of water.
2. 1 ½ bags of trail mix.
3. 5 packs of beef jerky.
4. 4 packages of tuna.
5. 8 protein bars.
6. Bandages, Band-Aids, and antibiotic cream.
7. 2 bottles of Benadryl.
8. Assorted foil packs of pills in a plastic bag.
9. 1 gun.
10. ½ box of ammunition.
11. 2 flashlights.
12. 1 long rope.
13. 2 boxes of matches (each in its own plastic bag).
14. 3 pairs of wool socks (This seemed like too much to me, but I didn't say anything.)
15. 1 rain poncho.
16. 3 candles.

The water was definitely a problem. We would need more. And the food situation was not great either.

Max wanted to eat a protein bar but Niko said absolutely not.

I felt stupid I hadn't grabbed a bag.

Niko didn't say anything, but there was a moment when he said,

26 MILES

'This is all we have? Out of everything on the bus?'

And I felt bad.

He'd packed it so well and now a bunch of mean thugs had it all to themselves.

Sahalia cried herself to sleep. She was curled on one of the banquettes.

Max, Batiste, and Ulysses went and lay down on the bed around Josie. They arranged themselves like puzzle pieces, fitting themselves next to her body as closely as they could. We were safe, but I think they wanted some extra feeling of comfort.

I took the other banquette, which was not comfortable at all, and used my very smoky sweatshirt as a pillow.

I woke up to the sound of arguing. I had missed the start of the argument. I had also missed the moment when Josie woke up, but it must have been quite a shock for her to find us not on the bus and learn she was type O and how Niko had drugged her and then about the cadets and Brayden.

It was Brayden she seemed stuck on.

'How could you leave him?' she demanded.

'Josie, I had a choice. Him or you,' Niko protested.

'He's wounded!'

'It all happened fast. I didn't have time to do anything.'

They were standing near the door. Just one candle was lit on the Formica counter, peach-scented, I think, and it gave them a glowing quality. I could just make out their shining silhouettes.

'After everything you said about not wanting him to die, you left him on a bus with a bunch of strangers?' she asked softly.

'I had no choice.'

'There had to have been a way, Niko!' Josie said.

I could hear the tears in her voice.

'Josie. Josie, please,' Niko pleaded.

Their voices became hushed. I craned my neck up to see. He had her by the arms and had drawn her close to him so their foreheads were touching.

'I promise I feel just as bad as you do,' he said.

And then they kissed.

Okay, that was new information.

I guess Niko and Josie were boyfriend/girlfriend now.

'We have to go after them,' Josie said.

'It's impossible. We have to go on. We have to try to make it to Denver.'

'But Niko—'

Suddenly he was close to shouting. 'You're the one who said we could do this! You said if anyone could get us to Denver it would be me!'

'And I meant it—'

'Well, now we've got to try,' Niko said. His voice was flat and gruff, the way it gets when he's serious. 'We've got maybe two days' worth of food and water if we really conserve and we're about 25 miles away. Jean told me she heard there is an Army camp about 10 miles down the road. If we get there, they'll help us.'

'What about the others?' Josie asked. 'The cadets are headed right for them.'

'Dean is smart,' Niko answered. 'That store is a fortress. He won't let anyone in. And who knows if the cadets will even make it there? Maybe they'll get ambushed.'

26 MILES

There was hopeful malice in his voice.

I had been thinking along the same lines.

'So we're driving, then?' Josie said. 'Can we find a car, do you think?'

Niko turned away from Josie and started repacking his backpack.

'Is that the plan?'

'No,' Niko said. 'I mean, the white stuff. It eats the tyres. That's why we didn't see any other cars moving on the road. So unless we can find one that's been inside this whole time . . .'

'We're going to *walk*?' Josie asked. Her voice was hard and incredulous.

'But don't worry, Josie, I can carry you.'

'What?'

'I'm going to sedate you and carry you. Or look for a wheelbarrow.'

Josie started to laugh.

'That's absurd, Niko.'

'I can do it. I can do whatever it takes to get you to safety, Josie!' he promised.

She shushed him and then she kissed him, pressing her body to his.

'If you're walking, I'm walking,' she said. 'I'll tape the gas mask down or something. I'll be very, very careful.'

'No, Josie,' he protested. 'It's not safe—'

She must have stopped him talking by kissing him on the mouth.

Josie whispered something to him. I think it was, 'I love you,' because then Niko said, 'I love you, too.'

I tried to go back to sleep. I didn't want to be a Peeping Tom or anything and they were making out pretty hard.

'Josie?' called Ulysses from the bedroom. 'Josie!' Then something in Spanish.

Maybe he was having a nightmare.

She moved to go comfort Ulysses.

'We're going to get these kids to safety, Niko,' she said and I could hear the smile in her voice. 'We can do it. You and me.'

What about me? I thought to myself.

And then I realized, maybe she was talking about me. Maybe she thought I was just one of the kids.

26 MILES

11 DEAN

AFTER A GOOD, LONG while. The rage receded.
I became aware that I was lying facedown on the
linoleum. I tried to move and the pain in my shoulders
and quads was unbearable.

I realized I was hog-tied.

Jake had hog-tied me.

I was groggy, and for a moment I just lay there.

Blood from my mouth was sticking my cheek to the
inside of the air mask. Slowly I used my tongue to loosen
the bond. I felt around in my mouth for broken teeth.
There were definitely a couple of teeth missing.

My glasses were gone. Broken, no doubt. Awesome.

I breathed in, taking a good long draw of the moist,
clammy air filtered into the mask.

Jake and Astrid came close, arguing.

'I'm telling you, I was walking around the store. I was going to try the intercom in the back when I heard the noise.'

'Why were you coming back anyway?' Astrid asked, her voice muffled through her own air mask.

''Cause I missed you. Why do you think? I felt terrible I left that way. I really did.'

'You probably just came back because you ran out of drugs,' Astrid hissed.

'That's not true.'

They were lifting and fitting the cement blocks back into place.

'Let's just fix the wall,' Astrid said through her mask.

'Where is everybody?' Jake asked.

'Oh, Jake,' Astrid said, her voice sounding sad. 'They left. Niko started up the bus and they're all trying to make it to Denver.'

'No kiddin',' Jake said. 'I didn't think he had the huevos to pull something like that.' He was trying to be jocular, but he sounded exhausted and spent.

I moved my head, shifting my body onto one of my shoulders. The stupid face mask they'd duct-taped to me was cutting into my jaw.

I groaned. The grogginess was wearing off. Listening to Astrid and Jake was bringing me back – mostly because I felt like I was spying on them. I wanted no more of *that*!

'You mean it's just you and Dean?' Jake asked.

'I'm awake,' I said. They didn't seem to hear.

DAY 13

'It's not just me and Dean. Chloe and the twins are here,' Astrid told him.

'Well, where are they now?'

'I told them to lock themselves in the Train,' Astrid answered.

'I'm awake,' I repeated, louder. 'Can you untie me?'

'Hey, killer,' Jake drawled, bending into my field of vision. 'How you feelin'?'

He nudged me with his foot.

My shoulders were on fire.

'Untie me!' I demanded.

'You gonna behave like a human being? You all done being a monster?'

'I'm fine,' I grumbled. 'And where did you come from, anyway?'

'I felt bad about the way I left so I was coming back. Then I saw that guy attacking the store. Then I saw you attack the guy. Man, that was something.'

He looked a little green remembering it. But through a face mask, colours are off. I might have been wrong.

'Lucky I came along when I did,' he drawled. 'You might have hurt my girl.'

I turned my face away from him, pressing it to the cold linoleum of the Greenway floor.

He was right.

That felt like the worst thing about everything that had just happened.

I *would* have hurt her.

He tossed Astrid his pocketknife.

'Here,' he said. 'Why don't you cut the booker free while I go let the kids out of the Train?'

I craned my neck to watch him go.

But he didn't head for the Train.

He headed for the Pharmacy.

After she sawed through the ropes, Astrid and I worked on repairing the wall.

She and Jake had put most of the bricks back in place. We were using plumbing caulk to fill between them and to fill the holes where the rocks had crumbled.

It wouldn't keep anyone out, that was for sure. But it would seal the air out.

Astrid told me that Jake had dragged the body away and then moved the palette loader so that it blocked most of the hole and it wasn't too visible from outside. She told me the palette loader had had its tyres stripped off and was just rolling on its wheel rims. That seemed weird. Was there some kind of rubber shortage outside?

Jake had also removed the battery from the machine so no one else would be able to use it against us.

I nodded.

That was good. Whatever. We would have to guard the hole, to make sure someone else didn't just push right through . . .

It was a mess.

'We can board it up,' Astrid said, as if she was reading my mind. 'We'll put up plywood. We can make it safe again.'

DAY 13

I could hardly look at her.

I knew she wanted to talk about Jake's return but I felt wrung out and miserable.

I had killed a man.

I had killed a man.

And I had nearly hurt Astrid.

As for Jake . . . Well, I was not happy he was back. Not at all.

It was stupid to even think about my chances with Astrid. But with him back, I knew they were down to nil.

And did I mention, I *killed* a man?

Then Astrid made a weird, choking sound.

I looked at her. She was grabbing her mask.

'Are you okay?' I asked.

'Can't breathe!' she gasped. Her eyes were wide and crazed – she was in some kind of panic attack.

She was clawing at her mask, gasping for air.

I dragged her away from the wall, back into the store, into the Home Improvement aisles.

'Look, it's okay here!' I said, gambling that the air would be clean enough – that we'd sealed the leak enough. I ripped my mask off, the tape tearing at my hair and skin. 'The air's okay.'

Astrid took off her mask and took in a long, ragged breath. 'I'm sorry,' she wheezed. 'I just started to think about Jake and I felt trapped and then I couldn't breathe –'

'It's okay,' I said. And before I'd even opened them for her, Astrid was in my arms.

'Oh, Dean,' she said, and she looked up at me. 'I feel bad for him but he's not the guy for me.'

And God help me, I kissed her.

Her lips on mine felt first as soft as rose petals. Then her lips parted and her mouth was hot and merged with mine. It was, ahhh, the best feeling I had ever felt.

The thing is, it was in me. The type-O aggression. It was there. I could feel myself getting more powerful with every breath, like my blood was growing stronger in my veins. It wasn't as strong as when I'd been outside, but I could feel the O was gaining force. Suddenly I felt certain that it was going to win and get me under its control, so I tried to push her away from me.

But Astrid Heyman took her two hands and grabbed my head by the hair and brought my face to hers and kissed me.

Her hands were all over me.

My heart – my brain – my soul knew it was wrong.

But my mouth wouldn't say no and my hands wouldn't stop touching her. Her back, her belly, her breasts.

My bloodlust wanted her and her bloodlust wanted me just as bad.

So there on the floor of the table linen aisle, we took each other.

It was better than anything I had ever felt, moving in her and through her. My soul and hers exploding inside each other. I don't know how to describe it. Or if I even should.

DAY 13

We were overcome with madness together. Overcome together.

I'm pretty sure Jake saw us.

In any case, by the time we came to our senses again – by the time we got our clothes back on and our masks back on and by the time I was thinking straight again – he was high.

He had let the kids out of the Train and they were ecstatic that he was back.

They were cooking s'mores over the camp cook stove. I could see the remains of a hot dog and baked beans meal.

Luna sat at his feet, wagging her tail blissfully.

Astrid and I were sweaty and mussed.

We took our masks off as we approached them.

A weird kind of lie, I guess. That we'd had our masks on the whole time. That we hadn't gone insane and had sex.

'Hey, you two,' Jake slurred, his back to us. 'I was so hungry, we just cooked up some franks and beans. I hope you guys don't mind.'

'The wall's back up,' Astrid said, bustling off her sweatshirt and tossing the air mask on the empty futon couch. 'We need to reinforce it, but it's pretty solid.'

'Look at my gal. She can do anything,' Jake said to the kids. 'I missed her so much! I missed you all, of course, but 'specially my gal, Astrid!'

'We missed you, too, Uncle Jake,' Caroline chirped.

She and Henry were toasting marshmallows over the blue butane flame.

'Look,' Henry said. 'I got mine perfect golden.'

'That's how our mom likes it, just golden with no burnt parts,' Caroline added.

'Takes patience, though,' Henry commented.

'And a steady hand.'

'I just like mine burned,' Chloe said, putting her marshmallow into the centre of the flame. 'Look – I'm the Statue of Liberty!' She held her blazing marshmallow up high.

'Careful!' Astrid snapped. 'You'll burn someone.'

'That's always the risk!' Jake said.

He looked up at us and his head lolled off to the side and he caught it and grinned even wider.

I'd seen him do that before. He was high.

'The air's fine here. No symptoms. Right, kiddos? Chloe's feeling just fine. We must be far enough away from the hole.'

'Come on,' Jake slurred. 'We got Stay Pufts aplenty.'

'I'm going to go change clothes,' Astrid said. 'I feel dirty.'

Jake watched her leave, a glassy look in his eyes.

'Sit down, Dean,' Jake called. 'Stay awhile.'

He was definitely high on the same stuff he'd been taking before. Jake turned to the twins.

'Henry, d'ya know what they say about assumptions?'

'What?' Henry asked, bright as a penny.

'Chloe, do *you* know?'

DAY 13

'No. What?' she asked.

'Assumptions make an ass out of *u* and *me*!'

They all thought that was hilarious.

'Dean knows what I'm talking about, don't you, Dean?' He elbowed me in the ribs.

'Jake, what are you talking about?'

'Here I am, assuming everything will be the way I left it. But of course, how could it be? I've been gone for, what, two days? Two frickin' days?'

'Is "frickin" the f-word?' Henry asked.

'Yep,' Jake answered. 'It sure is.'

'Told you,' he said to his sister.

Caroline yawned again.

'I think I'd better check your bandage, Caroline,' I said. 'And it might be time for your medication.'

'Aw, don't go,' Jake said.

He tried to clap his hand on my shoulder and missed somehow, toppling over.

The kids thought this was the funniest thing ever.

'Oh, Uncle Jake!' Caroline squealed. 'You're such a card.'

'Uncle Jake?' I asked. 'Why's he an uncle, all of a sudden?'

'We decided,' Henry said. 'Astrid's the mom and you're the dad and Jake's the uncle.'

Oh, boy. Why are kids so . . . *perceptive* all the time?

To tell the truth, I liked their idea of the perfect Greenway family. But their timing sucked.

'Yeah.' Jake laughed – a tinge of desperation thrown

in there. 'They got it. They got it right. I mean, really, that's about the long and short of it.'

He got to his feet. He was moving slow, like an old man. A drunk old man.

'Kids,' he said. 'You'll have to excuse me. But I'm so tired I feel like I could cry blood.'

And he staggered back into the berths.

DAY 13

12 ALEX

EVERYONE WOKE UP AROUND 7 (just like they would have in the store).

We all woke up hungry and Niko doled out 1/3 can of tuna for each of us and 1/4 of a power bar.

Jean was moved to generosity by this and gave everyone a can of Fresca.

Warm Fresca and dry tuna. Yum.

Sahalia let it slip that she had some gum, but wouldn't share it. Not one little stick. Fortunately, Jean let me rub some toothpaste around on my gums so I wouldn't have breath like I ate a donkey's butt all day.

I would have thought that we would all want to stay there in the trailer for as long as possible, but surprisingly enough, we do not.

I'm writing this last piece, then we're going. I think it was because it was so small in there. We were all on top of one another.

And when the kids heard that the Army guys are only 10 miles away, everyone got excited.

'We can make 10 miles no problem!' Max crowed. 'We can do 10 miles in our sleep!'

'*Yes, sir, that's my baby. No, sir, don't mean maybe!*' Ulysses sang in his Mexican accent. Where he learned that, I could not say.

'I don't know,' Batiste said. '10 miles is a lot.'

'It's going to be hard work, but I know we can make it,' Josie said, patting Batiste on the arm. She's always very encouraging for the little kids. I think that even if we were marching off a cliff, she'd keep everyone peppy and excited.

'But Max is staying,' Jean asserted. 'Baby, you're home now and I'll keep you real safe here with me. You're staying, right, pally?'

Max thought about it for maybe 3 seconds.

'No offense, Auntie Jean, but these guys is just as much family as you is.'

'But I'm a grown-up, Max! And maybe your dad'll come here looking for me!'

Max screwed up his face like he really didn't think so.

Jean got down on the floor and looked him right in the eye. 'This is your best chance, hun. You're staying!'

'Auntie Jean, you ever meet my dog, Lucky?' Max said. 'I had this dog named Lucky and he was a mutt what we found out back of the Safeway and he was missing one eye. And my dad says, "Aw, they did right to put him out with the trash, son. That dog's no good." But I swore and swore I'd take good care of him if they'd let me keep him and my mom said, "Over my dead body," and then my

26–22 MILES

dad said, "Maybe it's not such a bad idea," and that's around when my dad moved out. Anyway, I took Lucky to the free animal clinic and they sprayed him and gave me worm drops for him and also cut off his man parts. He cleaned up real good. But my mom still hated him. I don't know why.'

'Honey, all I'm saying is I want you here with me—' Jean tried to interrupt.

I guess she'd never heard Max tell a story. He just continued right on.

'So then for Christmas, my mom goes and gets me a brand-new puppy from the actual pet store. A Chow, real fluffy with a bow. And she goes, "You can keep this new one, baby, but you gotta let me take old Lucky to the shelter," and I said, "No way." Oh, she yelled and put up a fuss and said how do you not want this darling fluffy Chow and instead you want that mangy, stinky so-and-so.'

'I just think you'll be safer here—'

'And then she went and gave that Chow dog to her sister Raylene and played it off like she always had meant it to be for her anyways. Well, then on the last day of vacation, do you know what happened?' Max asked us all. 'I was walking in the lot behind the sewage treatment plant and Lucky starts barking his head off and what do I see? I'm about to step on a rattlesnake! It's just there sleeping over the slops tank, where the ground is nice an' hot and it's shaking its tail and hissing at me, and then Lucky rushes forward and bites the thing on its neck and kills it dead!' He looked at us, as if his story completely answered Jean's concerns.

After a few moments, she said, 'Honey, I don't understand that story. What does it mean?'

'It means stick with the dog you know, Auntie Jean,' Max told her. 'Stick with the dog you know.'

Niko wants us all to drink lots of water. He's made the point that the kids who need to keep their masks on will not be able to drink out there. I keep forgetting that, but he's right. If they lift their masks, they'll get a hit of the compounds and they could die.

Or Josie could turn into an O monster and kill us all.

Jean had the idea that we should take some cigarettes with us. Then we could get into a car and Sahalia and I could fill it with smoke and then the others could take off their masks to drink.

Sounds like a lot of work just to get a drink but it's what we'll have to do. We do not really need to be concerned with the harmful effects of cigarette smoke, at this point.

Jean gave Niko 3 packs, which is a pretty expensive gift.

All the while she was crying and made Niko promise if we get to help to send someone back for her.

We left the trailer park and followed the toll road.

Niko had us walk in this order: him, then Max and Ulysses, holding hands, then Sahalia, then me and Batiste, holding hands, then Josie at the rear.

It bothered me that I had to hold hands with Batiste, but I got used to it. And he was really scared, so it was a good idea.

Only Niko was allowed to have a flashlight. He was right, because when the little kids had them, they'd shine them all around and that was worse than not seeing around because every so often they'd find a body and then they'd scream and cry.

Niko kept his light on the ground. A few feet in front of us. Steady and measured.

It's hard to walk in the dark, but it was sort of okay, because it was like we had blinders on. We couldn't see to the left or the right, just where the flashlight was.

We didn't walk on the road. Niko felt we might be attacked.

Instead we walked on the side about 20 feet off, parallel to the road.

On the road were lots of cars and lots of bodies. Things were moulding over, the white fuzz growing in drifts over cars and bodies.

It made me think of Mr Culleton, in Earth Studies, and our block on composting. He said that in a compost pile, things returned to their most dense, nutritive form.

If the sun ever comes back, maybe this will be the best farmland ever.

I know that's a stretch, but that's the only nice thing I can think of to say about all the slime and mould.

Anyway, we walked.

And Batiste got blisters, which he told me, and he got thirsty, which he told me, and he got hungry, which he told me.

And I said, 'I'm sorry about that, Batiste,' every time and it actually seemed to help him. Then I'd give his hand a squeeze and that also seemed to help him.

It was a hard, hard walk.

Finally, Niko led us back up to the road. He started flashing the light into cars.

I nudged Batiste. 'I bet we're going to stop for a water break!'

He smiled at me, and squeezed my hand.

Niko flashed the light in a few cars, but there were bodies in them. He made us stand back from him and wouldn't let us look in.

I didn't mind standing back. I didn't need to see any more bodies and none of the little kids did either.

On some cars, Niko tried the doors but couldn't get them open.

Then, suddenly, he ducked down and motioned for us all to duck down. He cut the light.

A motorcycle was coming.

It darted and veered between the cars. The light seemed really bright and it made me realize that my eyes had become somewhat adjusted to the darkness.

It came closer and closer.

It was a biker guy wearing goggles – he had a long beard and a leather jacket and everything. And riding on the back was a little old man. He had a snow hat on and a jacket that seemed way too big for him.

They went right by and didn't see us at all.

'Maybe it's his father,' said Batiste.

'Most likely,' I agreed. 'Or just someone the biker found and wanted to save.'

He must have had the bike stored away somewhere airtight, like our bus.

I wondered how long the tyres on our bus had lasted. I hoped that they had rotted to shreds.

Niko found a car. It was a silver Nissan Murano.

He waved us over and we hurried and got into the car. Max and Ulysses flopped down in the way back. I sat in the backseat with Sahalia. Batiste and Niko and Josie were up front. Like a family car trip. Except not at all.

Sahalia and I got out the cigarettes and started puffing away.

Do you know how awful cigarettes are? The smoke gets in your chest and makes you cough. You do get a nice feeling in your brain. A kind of openness. But that's it.

I was blowing smoke towards the back and Sahalia toward the front.

'Is smoking a sin?' Batiste asked Niko.

'No,' Niko answered. 'It's unhealthy, but it's not a sin.'

'Then I guess I'll smoke, too.'

'Okay,' Niko shrugged.

'No fair!' Max and Ulysses protested.

Sahalia lit a cigarette for Batiste and passed it to him.

'Don't inhale too much,' she warned. 'Or you'll puke.'

I held my cigarette between my pointer finger and my thumb, but Batiste had his between his first two fingers – like a V. He looked like a little Frenchman.

Sahalia watched him for a second and then snorted with laughter.

Batiste pricked up one eyebrow and said, 'What?'

Somehow, that was just too funny.

Him all grimy, wearing God knows how many layers, but with a clean, round face and his hat perched on his head and the cigarette.

We all started laughing.

The laughing was that boiling-over kind. The kind that brings you to tears and makes you gasp for air.

When we stopped laughing I saw that Max had taken his mask off.

He seemed fine. He was laughing his head off.

Niko took off his mask and then Josie.

'It does seem to work,' Niko said, 'The smoke.'

'We'll all get lung cancer,' Josie said grimly.

This, too, seemed really funny and we all started laughing again.

Josie rolled her eyes and gulped down some water.

Niko handed out the protein bars.

'Thank you, God, for this food, amen,' Batiste said quickly before digging in to his bar.

'Niko, is it true what that cadet guy said?' Max asked.

'About what?'

'About them killing people at the airport,' he murmured.

'No chance,' Niko said. 'He was either lying or paranoid.'

'What's this?' Josie asked, concerned.

Niko explained what Payton had told us.

'If I could get my hands on that guy!' she growled.

She cracked her neck. Ulysses, watching her, started to whimper. His eyes looked dilated – not at all right.

'No. Nope,' she said. 'I'm starting to feel it. The smoke isn't working!'

Then she put her mask back on.

Max coughed and let out a cry.

The mitten he'd coughed into was bloody.

'Put your mask back on!' Niko shouted. Ulysses screamed, backing away from Max.

'You too, Ulysses! Help him!' Niko commanded Sahalia and me.

Sahalia and I tried to reach back and help Ulysses get his mask on but Ulysses batted at Sahalia's hands, crying out in Spanish.

Finally I grabbed him by the back of the collar and Sahalia got the mask on.

Max hugged his friend, pinning his arms down. 'It's okay, Ulysses. It's just us. It's just us.'

Ulysses calmed down after a few minutes.

So much for the smoky car idea.

But at least we'd gotten some water and a snack.

'Let's move out,' Niko said.

13 DEAN

I DREAMED OF ASTRID ALL night.

We hadn't spoken much after Jake went to bed.

Every time I looked at her, my face got painfully hot, so I tried not to look her way too often. She seemed to be giving me some space, too.

But after the kids went to bed, I had a thought.

'Hey, I'm worried about the gun,' I said.

'What gun?' she asked.

'Jake has the other gun. The one we got from Robbie and Mr Appleton. I'm scared he might get really depressed and . . . use it.'

'Oh God,' Astrid said, realizing my meaning. 'You're worried he has the gun and might kill himself?'

'I don't know him as well as you do, obviously. But those drugs are powerful.'

DAY 14

'Well, he doesn't have the gun,' she told me. She was studying her feet.

'How do you know?'

'He told me.'

'Well . . .' I exhaled, suddenly frustrated with him. 'Where is it? What did he do with it?'

Astrid let out a short, hard laugh.

'He gave it to some girl.'

And she edged away from me. She still wouldn't look me in the eye.

I started to feel bad, really bad, about what had happened between us.

I mean, dear God, had I forced her? She seemed as eager as I was, but in an O state, who knows. I had killed in that state – I was sure I could do a terrible thing to a girl.

Had I?

I felt sick.

And as tired as I was, sleep didn't come easy.

I always thought losing my virginity would be a life-changing thing. At the very least, I thought I'd feel relieved.

But instead of relief, I felt guilt and worry.

And, on top of it all, was there a chance we'd hurt Astrid's baby? I mean, ugh . . . I was in way over my head.

In my dreams I saw Astrid, saw her on top of me, naked and too golden and gorgeous for reality. Her belly glowing like starshine – growing moment by moment until it was huge and her cries of plea sure became cries of pain. Labour pains?

And in another dream I saw the guy with the pallet loader. I saw all the details I hadn't taken in while enraged. The look of fear in his grey eyes. The way he'd called for mercy.

And the two scenes got muddied up and it was Astrid I was cutting open and it was the guy with the loader who was in Astrid's belly.

And then Astrid was whispering on my neck.

'Wake up,' she said.

She was in my berth.

I shook my head awake.

I wasn't dreaming it – she was really there.

'What is it?' I asked. My heart was hammering wildly. Was it the wall? Jesus, we should have been watching the wall!

'I just want to talk to you,' she told me.

She had a pen-size flashlight pointed at the floor.

I saw she was wearing pink pajamas and had bare feet. She was shivering and she looked so beautiful I thought my heart might stop.

We went out to the Kitchen to talk.

I grabbed a fleece for myself, and for her a sweater I'd worn a few times.

We sat down at a two-top in the Pizza Shack.

I saw the brass fire pit Astrid had set up. It was shiny new and filled with a couple Duraflame logs. Somehow

DAY 14

the sight of it made me sad. It looked so shiny and hopeful.

'Astrid, I feel so bad about what happened,' I blurted out. 'It was wrong and if I had been stronger it never would have happened.'

'No,' she said with a wry set to her mouth. 'I knew you'd be feeling all guilty. Look, we didn't mean to do what we did but it's not bad or wrong. It's not even our fault. Jake and I had an open kind of thing – no commitment. We are free to do whatever we want.'

'Oh,' I said. I sat back in my chair. 'Okay.'

'The only thing I regret about what we did is that I think Jake saw us and I am worried about him. What you said about him committing suicide . . . I don't know. We need to watch him.'

She chewed on her lip for a moment.

Then she looked at me and smiled, glancing away. I think she was sort of blushing, even.

'But as for this afternoon? I thought it was . . . awesome.'

My heart had some kind of a seizure.

'But I . . . I feel like I forced you. Did I force you?' I said.

Now *she* looked shocked.

'No!' she exclaimed. 'Did I force *you*?'

'No, I mean, I wanted to do what we did. Very, very much. It's just . . .'

I didn't know what to say.

'Dean, can I ask you something?'

I blew out a big breath of air. I knew what she was going to ask.

'Was it your first time?'

The blush that hit me could have melted paint. I think I started stammering.

Astrid reached out and grabbed my arm.

'It's okay!' She laughed. 'Everyone has a first time.'

I tried to laugh, but I still felt really embarrassed.

'It's just not everyone who has a first time under the influence of a deadly chemical warfare compound,' she added drily.

'Yeah,' I said. 'It's gonna be hard to top it, frankly.'

We both laughed.

I scratched my head. I think even my scalp was beet red.

Then Astrid leaned over and kissed me.

It was a soft kiss. Her lips parted just a bit as she pressed them against mine.

I kissed back, my mouth feeling strong pushing against hers. She was answering me with her mouth and it was a quiet, sweet yes.

And then she pulled back gently.

'*That* should have been our first kiss,' she said quietly.

I sat for a moment, taking it all in.

'There's no reason why it can't be our first kiss,' I answered her. 'This could be, I don't know, the official start of Us.'

'Dean—' she started to protest.

'Astrid, you know how I feel about you. I'm crazy about you—'

DAY 14

'Dean, no. Not now.'

'Why? I'm good for you. You said it yourself, I'm a good guy. I would never leave you like Jake did—'

'Dean! Listen to me. If Jake confronts us, I'm going to say it was a huge mistake. I'm going to say it was just the compounds.'

'But why?'

'Look, maybe I have a little crush on you right now. But Jake's the father of my baby. *And* he's in really bad shape. He needs me. You said it yourself, he's depressed. He could be suicidally depressed! He probably needs the promise of . . . of being with me, if he's going to make it through this disaster.'

'That doesn't make sense.'

'It does to me,' she said.

'It's not fair!' I protested, probably sounding like a dumb kid.

She laughed bitterly. 'What about any of this is fair, Dean?'

Then she squeezed my hand.

'I'm sorry.'

And she rose to walk away.

I sat back in my chair.

'That's it? End of discussion?'

'For now,' she said.

It seemed *outrageously* unfair. When he was the king of the hill – the most popular, the most handsome – Jake got to be with Astrid. And now he was going to get to be with her because he was a pathetic mess.

When she liked *me*.

Me.

I stood up and headed back toward the berths.

No way was he going to win this one. I didn't know how it would play out, but I wasn't letting Jake get Astrid without a fight. And you know what, it felt good to have something to fight for, besides the old garden variety survival.

I couldn't get back to sleep so I made everyone a big breakfast.

A little crush on me.

Astrid had a little crush on me.

Was it wrong to feel a heart- spike of happiness in the middle of the Apocalypse?

I carried the food over to the Kitchen, and lit the fire in Astrid's fire pit.

The kids were excited when they saw the fire pit. It was something new.

They had stopped asking us about being rescued, I'd noticed. I'd stopped even thinking about being rescued. We all just stayed in the moment.

Jake came over, walking like he had a hangover.

He took a big bowl of oatmeal and a big mug of coffee with creamer.

Astrid came, dressed in my blue sweater and a pair of jeans. Was it some kind of message to me, the sweater?

Was I supposed to be placated by it?

DAY 14

The kids got their oatmeal.

'Cinnamon spice?' Chloe complained. 'Are we out of peaches and cream flavour?"

'If you can find it, you can make it for yourself,' I told her.

'Nah, I'll just eat this.' She sighed benevolently.

'Yeah, you're welcome,' I said.

'Jake, I have to tell you something,' Astrid announced. She sat down opposite him at the table.

Jake took the fireplace poker and jabbed at the Duraflame burning in the centre of the brass fire pit. 'Save it. I already know.' He scowled. 'I saw.'

'Saw what?' Caroline asked.

'It's not about that,' she said. 'That was just an accident. We're Os. It just happened.'

'What just happened?' Caroline asked again.

'I have news for you,' Astrid barrelled on. 'Good news.'

Jake set down his plastic spoon and looked up at her.

'We getting rescued?' he said bitterly.

'I'm pregnant,' Astrid said.

Jake just stared at her.

'What?' he asked.

'I'm going to have your baby, Jake.'

She pulled up her sweater – my sweater – and showed him her belly.

Jake saw the rise now.

Once you saw it, you couldn't miss it.

'How far?' he croaked.

'Four months,' she said.

'You're gonna have a baby?' Caroline gasped.

Astrid nodded. A smile played on her lips.

The kids squealed. They jumped up, so delighted. So happy. They hugged her and danced around.

Astrid laughed and let them have their moment, but her eyes kept flickering toward Jake.

Jake roared with happiness and jumped up. He swept Astrid into a big hug and kissed her.

I'd had enough.

I walked away.

'What's wrong with Dean?' I heard Henry ask.

'He'll be okay,' Astrid said, loud enough for me to hear.

Sure, sure, I'd be okay.

The girl I loved, who loved me back or at least liked me back, was going to get back together with her manipulative, depressed, drug-addicted boyfriend.

Also, the world as we knew it had ended and add to that the fact that I had killed a man. That one kept creeping up on me.

I went to look at the hole. I wanted to take down some shelf-boarding from the Accessories Department and put it up over the hole as a layer of extra protection.

That's when I heard the noise.

Something was rattling in the storeroom.

'Hello?' I called into the dark space.

I shined a flashlight around.

DAY 14

There was the shattered Operations Centre, with the useless panels that had once controlled our power, air, and water.

There were the two lifeless bodies near the wall in their matching floral shrouds.

Boxes of merchandise spilled their guts here and there.

Empty pallets in a messy stack against the gate, next to the intercom.

Everything was in its place.

The rattle came again and it wasn't coming from the loading bay gate.

It was coming from the hatch.

I stormed back to the Kitchen. They were all gathered there, lingering over the breakfast that I had cooked for them.

'Jake!' I shouted. 'Did you leave the ladder hanging down from the roof?'

'What?' Jake asked, looking befuddled.

'Did you leave the ladder hanging down from the roof when you left us, three days ago?'

'No,' he protested. 'Alex hauled it up after me. I'm not stupid and neither is your brother.'

'Well, there's someone up on the roof now. And they want in.'

'Who are you?' Jake hollered through the hatch. He had insisted Astrid take the kids to the Train. She had agreed, much to my surprise.

The hatch was padlocked, thank God. I had checked it the day before.

'We're just some kids,' the voice said.

It did sound like a kid.

'Please let us in. It's scary out here.'

Now, that sounded a little like sarcasm. Jake and I exchanged a look. We stood on the metal staircase, crammed together, under the hatch.

'How did you get up there?' Jake hollered.

'What?' the voice said. 'We can't hear you.'

Whoever he was, it sounded almost like he was laughing.

Jake and I shared an uneasy look.

'How the hay'd they get up there?' Jake murmured.

'We need to talk to you. We have a message from your other friends.'

'What other friends?' I shouted.

I'd put on a mask, of course, in case we decided to open the hatch.

'What other friends?' Jake repeated.

'The ones with the bus.'

I stared at Jake.

'You have to let us in!' the voice demanded. 'We have Brayden with us!'

Jake and I scrambled to open the lock.

Not for a second did we think it might be a trick.

'Brayden!' Jake screamed. 'How did you find Brayden?'

We pushed open the hatch, and three guys were

DAY 14

standing in the beam of our flashlight. They had guns.

They wore dark uniforms. Dirty and ragged. Their faces were uncovered. One of them wore a beret and had some gold cords going under his arm. He was the leader, there was no question.

'Hi!' he said, cheerful as could be. 'Thank you so much for letting us in!'

Then he kicked Jake in the chest.

14 ALEX

WE SET OUT AGAIN.
Max had to be carried. He had blisters on his feet that had burst. Niko had given him his extra socks, but apparently, Max's feet still hurt too much for him to walk.

I was sick of all the crying and whining.

I had blisters, too. Mine had burst, too. Every step was like little knives stabbing in my heels and I was hot in all the stupid layers. It occurred to me that I could just take them off. But then the little kids would whine even worse that it wasn't fair that I didn't have to wear layers, etc.

I had already paid the consequences of my blood type. I would never be able to have kids and I guess I would never be able to have sex. Wasn't that enough?

I was in a bad mood.

We trudged along.

Maybe a mile an hour? Maybe?

I was in a very bad mood.

It was less dark than usual and I realized maybe it was midday. It was almost as light as a night with a full moon. Or maybe it was that our eyes had adjusted to the light. But I could actually see, sort of. Everything was greenish, but I could see.

And then we stopped.

Niko crouched down, letting Max slide off his back.

He motioned for us all to get down, and as Sahalia and Ulysses crouched down, I saw why we were stopping.

Up on the road, under one of the floodlights, there was a soldier.

He was wearing lots of gear, including a machine gun.

Some equipment hung off his belt – 2 bright-orange air masks and some vial-shaped things in a holster. Flares, maybe?

Niko was whispering to us to stay put, but Sahalia lurched to her feet and started running toward him.

'Help us!' Sahalia cried. 'Hey, mister, please help us! Our friend is on a bus!'

'Wait!' Niko hissed, but Ulysses and Max started running toward him, too. 'Wait!'

The soldier turned and at first I thought he was smiling at us. He took off a hat he was wearing and threw it aside, his arms open wide.

Then he brought up his gun and I was running then, too.

He fired it at Sahalia!

It just went *CLICKA, CLICKA, CLICKA*.

And then he roared.

The soldier was O. Definitely O.

Sahalia skidded to a stop. She tried to back up but Ulysses crashed into her and then they were all scrambling backward, away from the soldier. He swung his gun free from his shoulder and started coming at Sahalia with it like it was an ax.

He said something. It came out a dry grunt.

He lifted up his gun and brought it down again.

Said the word again.

Niko grabbed Sahalia and hauled her back. Josie grabbed Max, and Ulysses and I ran.

I ran by Batiste, who was frozen in horror, and grabbed his arm and shouted, 'Run!'

The O soldier was right on us.

He kept grunting his word. And sometimes he would laugh this horrible, low guffaw that sounded like a cry of pain, but was his laugh all the same.

And then I understood what the word was.

He was saying, 'Kids.'

All I had in my mind was to get away. I'm embarrassed I didn't take more care of the younger kids, but all I did was run.

So, my mind wasn't working in a logical way but my theory, looking back, is that the Os who had been out the whole time since the compound leak were worn-out. All that rage had drained them.

The O soldier was still vicious and strong and deranged, but he looked thin and thirsty. The bloodlust must make them stupid, is my idea. Too angry to eat or drink properly.

The O soldier stumbled on the underbrush as he chased us.

His slowness was good for us because we started to get some distance on him.

Tall, thin shapes rose up through the dark air in front of us and I realized it was an aspen grove. The skinny trunks stood white and it was very still between them.

Now we dodged away from him like rabbits, going in different directions, and he got very frustrated.

Josie grabbed me and pulled me with her behind a stand of three trees.

The little kids headed for Niko, who started boosting Ulysses up into the thin branches of one of the trees.

Good idea, I thought.

The O soldier headed toward Max.

Sahalia, who was behind a different tree, shouted, 'Over here, dummy!' and waved. The soldier lurched toward her.

'Max!' Niko hissed, calling him. Niko was now helping Batiste into another tree.

Max moved toward Niko, but his boot got stuck in a root, I think, and the boot pulled halfway off. Max screamed and I realized his blisters were worse than I'd thought. I could see blood on his socks and the O soldier headed back toward him. Max couldn't get his foot free.

'Here!' Josie yelled, waving. 'You stupid jerk!'

She threw a stick at him but the soldier didn't turn.

'A KID, A KID, A KID!' the soldier repeated, his voice deranged and happy and disgusting.

He was descending on Max's cowering form. Max screamed.

And then Josie stepped in front of me, and as she moved toward the soldier, she took off her mask.

Just pulled it off and threw it to the side, like it was nothing.

As she ran, she breathed in big, loud breaths.

She launched into the air and landed on the soldier's back.

The sound she made as she flew at him was horrible.

It was loud and jagged and throaty. It was also joyful. Liberated.

Pure rage: 'WRAAAAAAAAAAUGH!'

It seemed like something she'd wanted to say for a long time.

Josie landed on his back and I think she sunk her teeth into the back of his neck. He made a motion to swipe her off and the motion toppled him to the side.

Max finally pushed back, away from them, scooting back through the dead leaves and dirt.

The soldier threw Josie off him. She rolled back in the leaves and hit her head on a tree.

'You gonna kill us?' she growled as she rose, her voice thick with hatred. 'A bunch of kids?'

They circled each other. Meanwhile, Niko dug in his backpack for the gun. Sahalia had come around the back of my stand of trees. She grabbed me to her. She clung to me, hugging me.

Josie launched forward through the air. Almost like flying. She tackled the soldier. He took a swing at her but missed.

'I can't get a shot. I can't get a shot!' Niko shouted, trying to aim the gun at the O soldier. His hands were shaking.

Then Josie was on top of him, sitting with her legs over his shoulders. She started punching the soldier on either side of his head in alternation. She was just whaling on him.

'Big guy?'

He was kicking, then more weakly.

'You kill kids?'

She lifted his head and banged it down. On a rock, I think, because there was an awful sound.

'You're tough?'

Again she banged down his head. Again the sick thud.

Again.

Josie grabbed the soldier by the hair and screamed in his bloody face.

'You kill kids, huh?'

Only he was already dead. His legs weren't moving and his face was splattered with darkness. His head, actually, seemed to not be the right shape any more.

'You gonna kill us?' Josie asked him again.

And another thud.

'He's dead,' Niko said.

She banged his head again.

'Josie, he's dead!' Niko shouted.

He dropped the gun and lurched forward toward her.

'No!' she shrieked, backing up. 'Get back!'

'It's okay, JoJo. You're going to be okay.' Niko tried to reassure her. He had his hands up, as if to show her he meant no harm.

Niko scrambled to the dead soldier's body. He pushed him over, scrambling to grab one of the high-tech air masks on his belt.

'Put a mask on!' Niko pleaded through his own. 'Let me get a mask for you! You'll feel better.'

Sahalia darted forward to try to help Niko get the mask.

'No,' Josie sobbed, backing up.

Batiste stepped forward.

'Josie, you saved us. It's over now.'

'Aaaaargh!' Josie cried. She wiped her bloody hands over her face.

Then she turned and ran.

'Josie!' Niko cried. 'Don't go!'

'Josie!' we all screamed.

But she ran away.

I think she might have killed us if she'd stayed.

Niko started sobbing.

There is no other word for it.

He just crumpled down over the legs of the dead soldier and sobbed.

I didn't know what to do. I sat down.

Sahalia went over and kind of rubbed Niko's back.

Batiste kept screaming for Josie.

Max was whimpering. He was in pain.

Ulysses climbed down from the tree and went and got Max's boot from where it had got stuck under the root, and for a long while, that's all the movement there was.

Just fat Ulysses, trying to help his friend get his boot on.

Then, Niko sat up.

He very methodically stripped the gun belt off the soldier's corpse. He took the high-tech air orange mask #1 from the belt, then took his own mask off and quickly switched, putting the better one on.

We could now hear his breathing. He was still having those leftover sobs. The sporadic ones. We could hear because the high-tech mask had some kind of a speaker built in.

Niko took the other mask over to Max.

He moved slowly, but purposefully, like someone chronically depressed or very, very tired.

'Hold your breath,' he told Max. I couldn't get over how well I could hear his voice. Like, better than if he didn't have a mask on at all.

He ripped Max's mask off and put the high-tech orange mask #2 in its place.

We could hear Max draw in a big breath. It sounded wet in there.

Max sputtered, and then he said, 'I'm sorry, Niko.'

I thought to myself that we all were.

And Niko said, 'I know.'

Niko stripped the soldier bare. He left him in his underwear but even took his socks.

The socks he put on Max, then he put the soldier's boots on Max, then he put the soldier's coat on Max.

To their credit, neither Batiste nor Ulysses said a word about fair.

Niko put the soldier's pants on over his own layers. I guess he thought they would be too long for Max.

The vials were flares and I got to wear the belt.

'I'm hungry,' Max said, his voice sounding small somehow. 'Is there any food?'

'We have to get somewhere safe,' Niko said. 'Then we'll eat and drink.'

'Like where?' moaned Sahalia.

'Another car?' Niko said.

There was something so bleak about his voice, even Sahalia knew not to press him further.

He walked and we followed.

Josie was following us.

I was sure of it.

There were sounds, coming from behind us. Snaps in the brush. Twigs breaking.

I was pretty sure.

Then I saw Niko perk up, after he heard the sounds, too.

'Niko, did you notice that Josie, even when in that enraged O-monster state, was able to form full sentences?' I asked him quietly.

'I didn't notice, but yes. I think you're right.'

'Dean couldn't speak that way when he attacked me,' I continued. 'Maybe Josie's—'

Niko held up his hand to shush me. And he whispered, 'Let's not talk about her. We might scare her away.'

Then his pace picked up some.

What Niko did next was a total surprise to me.

He told us a story.

'You know, we're probably not going to have to walk much farther.'

'Why not?' said Max in a thick voice.

'Mrs Wooly.'

'What do you mean?' asked Sahalia.

'She's out looking for us, of course.'

Sahalia snorted.

'Really?' Batiste asked.

'Of course,' Niko said. 'She's got a new bus, I bet. Or maybe a minivan. She's out driving around looking for us.'

'What's in the bus? Ulysses wants to know,' Max said.

'Well, it's a really nice bus. So of course, it has a kitchen stocked with food and drinks.'

'What kind of food and drinks?' Batiste asked.

'Um . . .' Niko thought for a moment. I had the sense his imagination couldn't quite keep up with his own narrative.

'There's a tray of sandwiches,' I joined in. 'With plastic wrap over it. Like from a deli. And there's potato salad and macaroni salad and pickles. To drink there's pop, but also fresh-squeezed orange juice.'

'You know what's cool about the bus?' Sahalia added.

I thought she'd say 'nothing.'

But instead she said, 'It's got beds in it. I'm serious. These white beds with clean sheets and fluffy duvets.'

'What are duvets?' Max asked.

'They're these comforters stuffed with feathers and they're incredibly soft and warm. Like sleeping under a cloud.'

'Well, where's she going to take us?' Max asked.

'I'll tell you where . . .' Niko said.

We walked for a moment as Niko thought.

'To Alaska,' he said. 'We're just going to drive straight there.'

It was good, to talk about something real.

I know that sounds stupid because, of course, what we were talking about was totally fantasy.

But one month ago, what would have been more far-fetched: a ride in a van stocked with sandwiches and beds, or a series of environmental catastrophes that would leave us in a dark world filled with corpses and monsters?

We talked about Mrs Wooly for a good long while.

No one bothered us or attacked us.

And every once in a while I caught the sound of someone trailing us.

And I was happy, because I knew it was Josie.

And Niko did, too.

15 DEAN

THE CADETS JUMPED DOWN onto us, forcing us backward down the staircase.

They screamed war cries and were laughing with the raw exhilaration true bullies feel.

Punching and kicking and pushing, they whaled on us as they pushed us down to the bottom of the stairs.

I fell to the cement floor, bashing my head and my shoulder. Something tore inside my shoulder. It screamed in protest, and I had trouble gathering up my body again. I felt jumbled and frozen with the pain of it.

I just lay back down on the floor.

'Zarember, go get Anna and the others,' the lead cadet ordered. 'Tell them the sweet little sissies opened right up for us.'

One of the two cadets started back up the stairs.

DAY 14

I saw Jake sit up, shaking his head to clear it, trying to recover.

'Mickey?' Jake said. 'Mickey Zarember?'

The figure on the stairs stopped and turned.

'Who are you?' he asked.

He had short brown hair and a huge bruise on one side of his face.

'Jake Simonsen. Remember me? I was a prospective at the Academy . . . I stayed with Jamie—'

'Holy crap, Payton,' Mickey Zarember said, coming back down the stairs. 'I do know this kid. Jake. He stayed with Jamie Delgado. This kid can hold his liquor!'

Mickey wanted to cross to Jake, you could feel it, but he waited for a nod from Payton. Payton did not nod.

He swaggered over to Jake himself.

'So we know you, huh, kid? Lucky for you. Pretty darn lucky.'

Payton gave Jake a hand and pulled him to his feet. He pulled Jake real close, right up to his face.

'Cadet Lieutenant Colonel Bradley Payton, squadron commander of the Fightin' Fourth,' he said. 'And you are?'

'Jake Simonsen . . . sir,' Jake answered, finding his footing.

'Pleased to make your acquaintance, Jake,' Payton said, his face just inches away from Jake's. Then he released his grip and Jake backed away a step and looked at the floor.

'I hope you got a lot of food, kid. 'Cause we're starving.'

'Yeah, totally, whatever we got is yours.' Jake grinned, the model of jocularity. 'We have more than we can use!'

I shot him a look.

Jake smiled right at me and I read total terror behind that smile.

There were five of them, including Payton, and a little girl. The girl was somehow wearing a white jacket that wasn't filthy. She looked strange and withdrawn.

'This is Anna. She's my niece and she's our little decoy. Our lucky charm.' Payton ruffled her hair. 'Like a rabbit's foot. Only don't touch her. Nobody touches her. It's one of our rules. That's because she's my cousin.'

The girl looked far, far away. She smoothed her hair down with utter detachment.

None of them had an air mask or was wearing any layers so that meant they were all either AB (paranoia) or B (sexual dysfunction). They had guns. Shotguns and handguns. Each one seemed to be packing something.

As they clattered down the staircase, my mind was racing a million miles an hour.

Could I somehow go out and warn Astrid?

Would she know to stay hidden and not come hollering to see what had happened?

Most of all, how were we going to get them to leave?

It was obvious that Payton was paranoid. He seemed crazy and very aggressive.

After he'd helped Jake up, Payton saw the wrapped-up bodies in the corner and went right over to them. I cursed myself for not covering them up.

DAY 14

Payton poked them with the barrel of his handgun.

'Naughty, naughty!' he said, wagging a finger at Jake. 'Somebody's been killing grown-ups! We're going to have to keep an eye on you. And your friend, too.'

What's your name, honey?' he said. He strode over to look into my air mask.'

'Dean.'

'Dean. I get it! Like the dean of a school!'

Payton was at least twenty, maybe twenty-one or twenty-two. Broadly built. His crew cut was brown and there were little dots of dried blood on his face. From a splatter that was not his own.

His eyes were the colour of yellow mud.

'Hey, Deano.' He tapped on my air mask with his gun. 'What are you, O or A or AB or what? Is that your handiwork over there?' He nodded toward the bodies in the corner.

'I'm A,' I lied.

'Well, then we'd better get you out of here before you start to peel, son.' He winked at me.

He turned to Jake. The last of his group were filing down the stairs.

'Well? Let's eat!' Payton boomed. 'Come on, Dean and Jake Simonsen, you two lead the way!'

One of the other cadets hauled me up and I cried out from the pain in my shoulder.

'Oh now, don't whine. I hate whiners!' Payton tut-tutted.

'Wait,' I croaked as the cadet manhandled me toward

the two main doors.

'What?' Payton shouted. 'What did you say?'

'Be cool, Dean,' Jake said, anxiety heavy in his falsely light tone.

'The hatch,' I said, talking loudly so I could be heard through my mask. 'We need to close the hatch.'

Payton looked at me as if he were seeing me for the first time.

'Brilliant! Yes! Of course we need to close the hatch. I like this kid. I like these kids, Zarember! Nice work!'

And he threw his arm around me.

My shoulder screamed, but I kept my mouth shut.

Jake and I walked them toward the Food aisles (and away from the House).

My every agonized step was a prayer for Astrid to get the kids and hide, hide, hide.

The cadets whooped and started tearing into the cookies and chips and crackers.

Jake and I thought we were forgotten for a moment. I took my mask off and rubbed at my face. My whole body was covered in a cold sweat.

It was stupid, but I was almost glad my glasses were lost and broken, somewhere outside near the palette loader. Maybe I looked cooler and tougher without them.

Instinct told me coolness and toughness had suddenly become survival qualities.

A cadet came and stood watch over us.

'Dude,' Jake said to the cadet. 'Aren't you hungry?'

DAY 14

The cadet clearly wanted to be eating but had his orders.

'Shut up!' he growled.

'We're not going anywhere,' Jake said, as friendly as could be.

'I said shut up before I have to put an end to your chatter with the end of my Smith and Wesson!' the kid snarled. He was shorter than us, with camouflage grease paint all over his face and through his hair. He also had a lame, scraggly mustache.

I nicknamed him Greasy.

We watched them gorge themselves, eating and drinking and spraying one another with soda.

If we hadn't seen the kids by now, there was a very good chance that Astrid had gotten them all into hiding, wasn't there?

Jake and I glanced at each other from time to time and that seemed to be what he was saying to me. It was definitely what I was trying to tell him.

And how the hell had Astrid managed to keep Luna quiet? I remembered reading something about mothers in World War II who'd had to smother their own babies to keep them from crying and revealing the position of the family to the Gestapo. I felt sick. How was she keeping Luna quiet?

'You guys made out like bandits!' Payton said, coming to stand with us. He held an open box of Chex mix. He offered it to us. 'You want some?'

'No, thank you,' I said.

'No, thank you ... ?'

'No, thank you, sir.'

'That's more like it. Listen, you don't know anything about us so let me elucidate for you. I am a second-class cadet. The rest of these losers are doolies. Fourth year. Like freshmen. That means I outrank them. That means they do whatever I say and then no one gets hurt!'

He threw his arm around me and I saw stars. I whimpered a bit and Jake shot a look at me.

'You know what I realized,' Jake said. 'I never asked how you guys met Brayden.'

Payton looked blank for a moment and then he laughed.

'Effin' Brayden. Oh Lord. He wants to know how we met Brayden!' he shouted to the gorging cadets. 'We met him on the bus.'

I felt my insides turn to ice.

'What bus?' Jake asked, bluffing.

'We ambushed the bus, Jake, don't play stupid. We ambushed the bus and that's how we found out about this place. One of the little squirts told us exactly where to come.'

Oh my God, he was about to say that he'd killed my brother? What would I do? What would I do if he said that?

'We told them not to leave,' Jake lied.

He was sweating. Jake was shaking and sweating.

'Stupid idiots! Why would they ever leave here?' Payton agreed. He munched another handful of Chex.

DAY 14

'Oh, I know. They wanted to save Brayden. Well, he died.'

'Yeah?' Jake asked.

'To tell you the truth, we killed him. He kept moaning and moaning. Oh Lord, it was driving me *crazy*. So I had to ask one of my guys to smother him. I couldn't take that moaning anymore. I hate moaners.'

Payton looked sidelong at Jake, assessing his reaction indirectly.

Jake nodded. 'Me too.' He looked grey.

'They never would have made it to a hospital anyway,' Payton continued. 'Nope, we kicked those losers off the bus. I believe they were going to try to make it to Denver on foot. Idiots.'

My brother, Niko, Josie, and the rest were now on foot. Or had been, whenever this ambush had happened. I felt sick to my stomach.

'But you know what, I made a mistake when I let them go,' Payton said. He looked around the Food aisles, and saw that Anna was drifting away toward the nuts and trail mix – out of ear shot. 'I should have kept that sweet little girly on the bus!'

Payton elbowed Jake.

'I bet you miss her right?' he said to Jake. 'Did you have yourself a little goodbye party before she set off?'

He was talking about Josie or Sahalia.

So he hadn't killed them and he hadn't messed with them.

That was good.

Okay, okay, Astrid *had* to have the kids hiding by now. She was very good at hiding away. They had to be safe from this sicko. I was starting to think he wasn't crazy from the compounds. He was just crazy on his own.

'Mr Payton, sir,' I stammered.

'Cadet Lieutenant Colonel,' he corrected me. 'What?'

'I've been meaning to ask. How'd you guys get up on the roof?'

'Old-fashioned grappling hook, Dean. That Zarember can climb anything. Then he found a ladder and threw it down for us. Real thoughtful of you to leave it up there,' he said, clapping me on the shoulder.

I should have kept my mouth shut. I almost fainted from the pain.

'All right, doolies,' Payton said, addressing the group. 'Spread out and give me a report. I want full recon on this here Greenway superstore. Exits, entrances, assets, liabilities, weapons . . .'

Payton winked at us.

I hated those mean, malicious winks.

'Also be on the lookout for any alcohol! Daddy could sure use a drink!'

The cadets cheered.

'Hey!' Jake said, as if suddenly remembering something. 'Where are my manners? Do you guys want to get high?'

DAY 14

16 ALEX

EVENTUALLY, WE SAW A development. Most of the houses were dark, but there were lights in a few.

'Can't we try one?' Sahalia asked. 'Maybe they have food.'

Niko didn't answer. He started to skirt the complex.

'Niko, please, can we rest?' Max said, starting to cry. 'Please?'

'Okay, okay. Let's try that one,' Niko whispered to us, pointing to a unit at the side of the development. Two windows had lights on in the first floor. The light was diffuse, like it was coming through sheets of clear plastic.

'Stay close,' Niko said.

So we all came in close up behind him.

And that was actually a mistake. Because it looked like a stretch of lawn ahead of us. A manicured lawn with some leaves and debris scattered around. But it wasn't.

I was right behind Niko, and suddenly he fell forward and the ground was jerked away from under my feet and I fell backward and I was falling back on Sahalia who was behind me and then we hit the bottom.

We were in a pit and above me I saw Ulysses holding on to some roots or rocks or something.

But he couldn't hold on very long and he tumbled down and landed with us at the bottom.

It was a trap.

Dean, we fell into a pit trap.

They had laid a tarp on top of part of the foundation for a new house.

Because it was dark, we didn't see the tarp and now were in a pit.

The walls were cut by an excavator. They had that pressed-in texture, with rocks and roots sticking out in places. The floor was just deep, sludgy mud. It was wet with water on top of the clay and with lots of putrid-smelling, rotting leaves and there was some of that white mold growing against the wall.

We were in one corner of an L-shaped pit.

If Niko had walked 2 feet to the side, we would have missed it entirely.

We were crying, screaming, I don't know, making the sounds of terror and surprise you make when you find yourself fallen into a dark pit.

'Calm down, everyone,' Niko commanded. 'Calm down!'

Everyone tried to stop crying. I tried to stop crying.

'We can get out,' Niko said. 'We can get out if we keep calm and work together.'

17 MILES

And then there was the light-swipe of a flashlight at the rim of the pit.

Yes, it was a flashlight and it was bopping around.

'Hello?' Niko called.

We all joined in calling hello, help, etc.

'Oh my God, Dad! We did it!' came the voice of a kid. 'I knew we'd catch someone! I knew it!'

'Settle down, Eddie, we don't know who all's in there.'

'Help us!' Batiste screamed.

Then the flashlight flashed down on all of us.

'Jesus,' the man said. 'It's a bunch of kids.'

'We're just trying to get to Denver. We're not trying to rob anyone or anything,' Niko said.

'Oh yeah? Well, we're not going to Denver. We're waiting this thing out, right, Dad?' the kid named Eddie said.

I hated this Eddie, sight unseen.

He's the worst person I ever met.

1. He had laid a trap for us.
2. We had fallen into the trap.
3. He still had a dad.

'Yeah, yeah,' said the dad. 'Well . . .'

'Give us your food and water and we'll let you go!' the boy shouted.

'We can't!' Sahalia shouted. 'We'll die without it!'

'Give it up or you can't get out,' the kid repeated.

'Now, Eddie, I don't know . . .' mumbled the dad.

We couldn't see them at all. Not with the flashlights shining right in our eyes.

Max started to whimper. 'The water's getting in my boots,' he whined.

'Look,' Niko said, his clear, digitalized voice going up to them. 'Maybe this seems like a game to you. Trying to trap people and take things from them. But we're going to die if you take our supplies. Do you want to be responsible for the deaths of six kids? Max and Ulysses are 7 years old, for God's sake!'

They had to let us up.

The lights went out of our eyes and we heard them arguing.

'Dad, we need the water!'

'But I didn't think they'd be kids—'

'What about Mom? She needs the water! Dad! I'm so thirsty!'

It was clear who the boss was in their family – Eddie. The meanest kid in the world. We couldn't hear the argument as well then because Max started crying hard. The water was burning his ankles and feet. Then a light shined back down and the man said, 'I see your point, son. The thing is, if we don't get your food and water, we're gonna die.'

Max's cries turned into wails, but then I heard a vicious shriek. It made me feel elated and sick to the stomach at the same time.

Josie's war cry.

And the lights went off us and we heard the fight.

She attacked the dad first and had him down and I guess was pounding on him. Then I think the son tried to hit her with something. There was a *thwack* and then the kid was crying, 'No, please, don't.'

And then Josie roared at him, 'GO ON THEN!' Her voice sounded like a monster but she let him go. 'GO!!!'

17 MILES

As much as I hated the kid, I didn't want him to die. And more than that, I didn't want Josie to be the one to kill him.

And the dad? Was he . . . ?

I heard sobbing then. Josie's voice, ragged and desperate

And then the sound of her standing up in the mud.

'Josie! Josie, it's not your fault!' Niko shouted. 'You can stay, Jojo. You can stay with us!'

'I can't,' said Josie, dark and tortured above us.

'Josie!' Niko cried. 'I love you, don't go!'

And then nothing.

She was gone.

After a few minutes, the boy came back.

'Dad?' he said. 'Daddy . . . Daddy?'

Then the light shined down again on us.

'You give me an air mask!' he shrieked. 'You throw it up right now!'

He started pelting us with rocks and clumps of mud. 'You give it now!'

The thing is, we did have an extra. We had three extra.

Niko wasn't speaking or moving or anything.

'Hold on!' I shouted. 'Hold on a minute!'

'I won't hold on! You throw one up now so me and my mom can get out of here or *I'll bury you alive!*

That just didn't seem like a credible threat, actually. He couldn't have been more than 11 years old and where was he going to get the dirt? But I didn't blame him for thinking illogically. His father was dead.

'We will throw one up if you let us out!' I shouted.

'What?'

I tried to think like Niko.

'We will throw up an air mask if you put down a rope for us.'

'Fine,' he spat. 'Throw up two, then.'

'Okay,' I bargained. 'But first the rope.'

'No way. First, the masks.'

'How about I throw one mask, you put down the rope, then I'll throw the second?'

The boy hesitated. 'Okay,' he agreed reluctantly.

'He won't throw down a rope,' Sahalia scoffed.

'The mask is an extra,' I said with a shrug.

'We're going to die down here,' she said.

Niko just stood there.

I took Niko's old mask, the one he'd used before he got the good Army one, and pitched it up.

'Now give us the rope,' I yelled.

The boy, Eddie, leaned over the edge, shining his own flashlight onto his face so we could see him.

'I hope you all rot in hell!' the kid said, his face covered with tears and snot. 'Your friend killed my dad!'

And he left, sobbing.

Niko took the gun out from his backpack.

'Niko?' I asked.

He looked at me blankly.

'Niko?' I asked again. He was acting scary.

He aimed the gun in the air.

'HELP!' he shouted. And fired *BANG*.

'Stop!' I yelled. He was scaring me. He was scaring everyone.

17 MILES

'HELP!' *BANG.*

The kids were screaming.

'HELP!' *BANG. BANG. BANG.*

'Niko, don't!' I screamed.

But he didn't listen. He fired our last shot and then he pitched the gun out of the pit and up onto the slimy grass above.

During all this, Sahalia had just lain down in the dank mud and was weeping.

'Get up,' Niko told her.

'It's no use. We're going to die.'

'No, we're not. Get up,' he said through gritted teeth. 'I'm going to give you a boost and you're going to go get a ladder.'

'I can't,' she moaned.

But he did get her up.

First, he tried that thing where one person steps into the other person's hands. But she was still 4–5 feet short of the edge.

Then he tried putting her on his back. Still way short.

So then they tried that again, but then I was supposed to climb up their bodies somehow and get on top of Sahalia's shoulders, but that didn't work. I couldn't climb up Niko. I just grabbed fistfuls of his clothing and pulled him backward until Sahalia fell backward.

'It's no use!' she screamed. 'We're going to die!'

'What about the flares!' I shouted. 'We can shoot up some flares and maybe someone will come and rescue us.'

'Or kill us!' Sahalia spat.

'It's worth a try,' Niko said after a moment.

I wiggled one of the flares out of the belt. It was sealed in a plastic wrapper with a white string hanging off. I pulled the string, and a scored middle section ripped open.

The flare was cardboard and there was a cap with a sandy surface on it.

I studied the flare. It was essentially a large, fat match, complete with a sandpaper striker attached to the cap.

But before I could light it, Sahalia gestured for me to hand it to her.

'I'll do it,' Sahalia said. 'I've done it before. And if you do it wrong too many times, it won't light.'

I handed her the flare. I had wanted to light it, but if she was showing an interest in our survival again, I thought I should encourage it.

She struck the cap against the tip of the flare.

Then the red light sparked up and molten light spewed out of the end. Sahalia held the flare as far away from her body as she could.

Neon orange light lit her up. I will never forget the sight of her there, her balaclava pushed away from her face, her long hair peeking through. Wearing a yellow slicker over her five layers. Ulysses and Max cowered behind her, each hugging the other for dear life, faces obscured by their air masks. Batiste's form just behind them, bent over and sobbing. Mud and grime all over them, and her, and roots and rocks jutting out from the sides of the pit.

'Should I just, like, throw it?' she asked.

Niko took it from her and hurled it up, over the side of the pit and out onto the grass.

Niko wrapped Max up in the tarp to try to keep any more water from getting to him. The wet was burning his legs and feet now and he kept making this low, animal kind of moaning.

17 MILES

Then Ulysses started praying in Spanish and Batiste started praying in English.

And then it started to rain.

That's when Sahalia asked me for my book.

Here is what she wrote:

My name is Sahalia Wenner.

It looks like we're going to die and I wanted to write this in case anyone finds it. If you do, please deliver my letter to Patrick Wenner, 106 McShane Place, Monument, CO.

Daddy, I'm sorry I wasn't a better girl for you. If I could go back in time I'd be up in the morning, helping you to make breakfast and do the dishes when you asked me to. I didn't know how good I had it and that's the truth.

I don't know why we had to fight all the time. I don't know what I was so mad about, now. I really can't remember.

I want you to know that after the hailstorm I was in the Greenway. Right there in our town. I don't know where you got to, or if you're even alive. But I was there with all these kids and I love them all now like they're my own brothers and sisters.

I fell in love with a boy there and now he's probably dead. I think you would have liked him, but I don't know. His name was Brayden Cutlass and he had the most beautiful brown eyes.

I wish I could have been a fashion designer or a singer like I wanted to. I wish I could have lived a life where I moved to LA and made my dreams come true. But that's not the world any-more – those dreams are dead now. Most of all I wish you find this, Daddy, so you can know that I love you so much and all I can think of is how much I wish you knew that. I guess maybe you're dead already and you already know what's in my heart.

Or maybe you knew all along. That would be the best thing. Better than I deserve. If somehow you knew all along how I really feel about you.

Love, from your girl,

Sahalia

Here's what everyone else wanted to say:

Batiste: 'Mother and Father, if I die, I will wake up in Heaven and maybe I'll see you there. Love, Batiste'
Max: 'Mom and Dad, I'm sorry I didn't find you. Be good and don't fight.'
Ulysses: 'I am Ulysses Dominguez.'

Niko wouldn't tell me anything to write.
'Stop writing in that book!' he yelled. 'We're going to get out of here. Let's light more flares. Someone must be out there.'
He lit and threw a red, another red, and a white.
We waited and the rain started seeping in through our layers.
A little while later, Max threw up.
He threw up inside his air mask and there was a lot of blood.
'Help us!' Sahalia started to scream. 'Somebody help us!'
We still had his old air mask and so now we had to try to switch it out.
Niko didn't need to call me over. I knelt next to Max and prepared to help.

17 MILES

Sahalia was still screaming her head off and her voice was going raw and hoarse.

'Hold your breath, buddy,' Niko told Max, but he was gasping and choking.

Niko took the air mask off. Max's face was a mess. Red, splotchy blisters all over the area around his mouth and nose and eyes and blood dripping from his chin.

I pressed the new air mask over his face and he gasped in.

The sound was muffled.

It was a horrible sound.

Max was going to die.

Niko gave an anguished, frustrated cry. Then he jumped up, like he'd been stung into action.

He turned to me.

'Here's what we're going to do. I am going to throw you up and you'll grab on to the edge and scramble out.'

'Okay.' I shrugged. I was crying.

Max was going to die.

Niko made that cradle with his hands and I put my foot in and he tried to heave me up. It took a couple tries to get the angle right.

I got up pretty far on the fifth or sixth try.

Grabbed some grass out over the edge, but it was so slick.

I wanted to keep trying, but a root scratched me in the face and I was bleeding.

Niko started to pray.

I didn't want to see that.

'Oh God,' he said. 'Please, God, please send us some help because I can't do it alone!'

Sahalia leaned forward and hugged Niko, her body pressing down on his, and I went too and there were two groups then: Sahalia, Niko, and I; and Batiste, Ulysses, and Max.

And then . . . then came a tiny 'Hey!'

An old voice. But mad.

'Who set off these flares? Hello?'

Then we were clamouring. I jumped up.

We all hollered and yelled but Niko yelled at us, 'Be quiet! BE QUIET! IF YOU WANT TO LIVE, SHUT UP!'

Then, Niko shouted up. 'We've fallen in a pit. Don't come too close or you might fall in!'

'I won't fall in! I'm not stupid,' came the voice.

Then a blinding light flashed down on us, going from one kid to the next.

'Jesus Christ,' the voice cursed. 'You went and fell in the foundation?'

'This family made it into a trap!' Sahalia snarled. 'They laid a cloth over it and trapped us!'

Niko shushed her.

'Please, if you could just help us out. We're a bunch of kids and one of us is really hurt.'

'The Mandrys. That's who set the trap. Looks like one of them got the tar beat out of him, too, by the look of it up here.'

'Yes, a girl named Josie did that,' Niko said.

'She's O,' I shouted.

'Looks like Tad Mandry's dead, here.'

'Please, mister, can you help us out?' Niko called.

'Well, I'm not a savage!' he shouted. 'Of course I'll help you. There's a ladder right here, for heaven's sake.'

17 MILES

There was a ladder up there? *Right* there?

'I'll help you out. But that's all. Now you all shut up and give me a moment,' the man said. 'We don't want to be attracting attention these days. Could be any number of nutballs out here.'

We huddled together, excited and relieved and still terrified of everything. The only sound was Max moaning and crying. And Ulysses and Batiste sniffling, I guess.

Then we heard a wet, sliding sound. It was the man sliding the ladder across the ground.

'That's it,' Niko called softly.

'I know!' the man grouched.

Inch by inch, we watched the ladder poke farther and farther into our air space.

'It's taking long because I'm old,' the man said. 'I'm too damn old for this nonsense.'

The ladder started to tip.

'It's going to fall, now. Watch out.'

'We're clear,' Niko called.

The ladder wobbled for a moment and then came crashing down.

The man was tiny. He was maybe the same height as Ulysses.

I couldn't see his face because he had a red-and-black-checkered scarf wrapped around it. By the way he moved, you could tell he was very old.

He helped Sahalia out first and then she turned and helped us one by one.

Niko came up last, carrying Max.

He slung Max onto the wet, muddy ground.

There was the body of the dad. He was lying on top of a rock. He'd fallen on it during his fight with Josie and he must have broken his neck, because his head was cocked to the side and he was looking up at the sky with an open mouth, like he was stargazing.

But, no, he was not looking at the sky. He was dead.

The earth was torn up in places, mishmashed with footprints and some dark brown-black slicks that were most likely blood.

'All right,' the man said. 'Good luck to you then.'

And he started to shuffle away.

'Please,' Niko said. 'We need to get somewhere safe so we can take care of our friend. And we need somewhere safe to rest.'

'Well, I can't help you!' he spat.

'But we're so thirsty,' whined Batiste.

'And Max is so sick,' Sahalia added. 'Please, mister. Please.'

And we all started in, begging him. 'Please, please, please.'

'I knew I shouldn't have come over!' he growled. 'I just came up to take out the trash, see? And then I saw the flares and I thought to myself, "Ignore it, Mario. You're gonna get sucked into helping someone and it will be a strain on your resources." But here I am.'

We must have looked a pitiful sight to him. All of us wearing filthy, matted layers of grimy sweatsuits. Me, Sahalia, and Batiste with our faces uncovered, coated with mud, the only clean parts being the trails made by crying. Niko standing with his head hung. Max lying, moaning, on the ground, wearing a bloody air mask. Ulysses clutching Max in the mud.

'I'll give you a day and a night. That's it!' he snarled. 'Some basic medical to fix you up the best I can. 3 meals and 1 night's sleep. But that's it. You have to swear you go after that.'

17 MILES

Niko stuck out his hand and said, 'We swear.' They shook.

Everyone started thanking him and Sahalia hugged him.

'Follow me then, and keep quiet about it,' he grouched.

He led us across the street, toward a smaller development we had already passed.

'What's he got now? Burns?' the man asked Niko, who was carrying Max.

Max was whimpering with Niko's every jostle.

'Blisters,' Niko answered.

The old man was hurrying as fast as he could. But old people walk slow. He led us toward a house. It was that pretend-English style, with the wooden beams. Trying to look like a Shakespearean house.

I thought we were going inside, but instead, he kept on going.

He went across his back lawn to a little building. It looked like a garden shed. A little too big for a garden shed, but that's what it looked like.

We went in and there were tools hanging all along the walls.

'Come in,' he crabbed at us. 'Shut the door behind you, for God's sake. This is a secret place.'

I couldn't read Niko's expression through his air mask, but I was worried. Did the old guy think we would be safe in a garden shed?

Then Mario bent over and picked at the edge of a rubber mat on the floor. It looked like a welcome mat, sort of, but old and scuffed up.

He lifted it and there, underneath it, was a metal handle sunk into the floor and a seam.

He pulled up on it but he was winded.

Sahalia and I stepped in to help.

'Hold on, hold on a minute,' he said. He addressed us. 'When the door opens, go right on down the stairs. They're steep, so mind you don't fall. Keep going so you're out of the way for the next person. All right. Go,' he told Sahalia and me.

We pulled up on the handle.

It was really heavy for the first moment, then a hydraulic lift kicked in and it rose up by itself.

Up above, everything was grimy and dirty and dark, but pure white poured up from below that door.

It was blinding, so used to the dark were our eyes.

'Go on now!' Mario ordered. 'Get below.'

We did not worry for a second that he might be tricking us or trapping us. He had so clearly *not* wanted to help us. Why would he be tricking us now?

And he wasn't.

As crabby and crotchety as he was, I trusted him right away. I think everyone did.

And we were right to.

He saved our lives and his name was Mario Scietto.

17 MILES

17 DEAN

'I GOT A PHARMACY FULL of Robitussin,' Jake bragged to Payton. 'We had some whiskey, but I drank it.'

'I like you more and more, Jake. I am glad you're considering entering the academy. You should do it,' Payton asked. 'I'll get you in my squadron. Would you like that?'

'Sir, yes, sir!' Jake responded.

Payton turned to the cadets, who were still awaiting his orders.

'Well, you heard me. Fan out! Use your lights and be thorough.'

So how much respect did I have for Jake? Before this . . . meh. Not very much. I *liked* him. You *had* to like Jake, because he was an affable, charming guy. Everyone liked Jake. Even when I hated his guts and wanted to kill him, I *liked* him.

But with the drugs and the way he just got so lost and depressed and the fact that he'd left us? Well, he'd fallen really far in my eyes.

Now, seeing him play this game with Payton and watching him carefully bluff and negotiate his way through this nightmare – he was kind of my hero.

My shoulder was out. Every step was agony for me. I wasn't going to be able to fight these guys. If we were going to make it through this alive, Jake would be the one saving us.

'Too bad you have no lights,' Payton said. 'Kind of grim in here, all dark like this.'

'Yeah,' Jake said. 'But we got a lot of flashlights. And, hey, you should see our campfire!'

Jake led Payton to the Kitchen.

I got his strategy. With the fire going, it looked right. It looked cozy and cheerful. You could believe that it was our campsite. As long as they didn't look for our beds.

The cadets started coming back, listing what they'd found. Greasy found the chainsaws and the patched hole in the wall. A thin, twitchy guy they called 'Jimmy Doll Hands' reported in on the water and remaining drinks near the Food aisle (and, yeah, his hands were weirdly small). They were fairly thorough. Zarember even found and reported on the oil stain on the linoleum and the tyre marks from where the bus had stood before it left.

But somehow, they didn't see the House.

DAY 14

The last cadet came back to report, a strong, burly black kid named Kildow. He looked like the most menacing of the cadets and carried a semiautomatic. At least, I think it was a semiautomatic. I'd only ever seen them in adventure movies.

Was he going to say he'd found the House? If he did, Jake could still play it off – like he was going to tell Payton, but hadn't gotten around to it.

Were Astrid and the kids hiding there?

I hoped they were up in the roof tiles by now . . .

'Anything to report?' Payton asked Kildow.

'Nope,' he said. 'Except a lot of crap in Tupperware in the back corner. I mean crap, literally.'

'Aw, sorry about that,' Jake said. 'That's the Dump.'

'You sure you don't have a girl or two around here?' Payton asked.

'You saw our girls,' Jake said sadly. 'They went and left us.'

'Well, all right.' Payton sighed, throwing himself down in a berth. 'Let's party, I guess.'

How do you throw a party for five crazy air force cadets and their mascot little girl in a superstore with no electricity?

Rekindle the fire in the fire pit.

Cook up some Jiffy Pop on the flames.

Crack open a couple dozen bottles of Robitussin.

That is what we did.

* * *

'Your arm's all wrong,' Payton observed, examining me across the fire.

'I hurt my shoulder when I fell,' I said.

'Let me see that,' Payton said. He got up and came over to me. I was sitting in a booth, my back to the wall. 'I can set it for you.'

'No, no, please. I'm okay,' I said.

I tried to catch Jake's eye. He was off telling Greasy and Zarember about what the earthquake was like in the store.

'Don't be a sissy,' Payton said. 'It'll only take a second.'

'It's fine,' I lied.

Dear God, I prayed, please keep this thug off me.

I was scared he'd make it worse and it already hurt more than anything I'd ever experienced.

'Come on, it's just a little pop. Zarember, Kildow, get over here.'

'Please, please, please no!' I shrieked.

Payton grabbed my hair and brought his forehead up to mine.

'Look, Dean. I know you're scared. I respect that. And you think I'm going to hurt you. But I'm not. I'm going to help you. And once your shoulder's back in the socket, you're gonna be grateful. And that's how I'm gonna get you on my side,' Payton murmured to me.

'See? It's not even about you, really. It's about this gang. My little gang of cadets. See, we're recruiting!' He threw his arms out wide, like he'd announced a new national holiday. The cadets cheered.

DAY 14

'I'm gonna recruit you by setting your shoulder, Deano. I'm going to take care of you and Jake. You're my doolies now! Get him up,' he commanded Kildow and Zarember. They hauled me to my feet.

'Please, don't,' I begged. 'You don't need to set my shoulder! I'm recruited! Please.'

But he pulled my arm so that my elbow bent and it was at a ninety-degree angle. He pushed my hand toward my other arm, across my body, then away, then toward it again while I screamed and my vision went electric and then God had mercy on me and everything went black just as I heard a *POP*.

18 ALEX

THE STAIRS WERE WHITE, with black scratch pads on each step to keep you from slipping. Sahalia went first, then me behind her. At the base of the stairs was a series of plastic sheets hanging from the ceiling. The long plastic pieces hung down like a fringe. We stepped through them. Lights automatically went on as we entered.

We were in an underground bomb shelter.

It was a long, skinny space, like a train car. We were standing at one end of it, in a sort of living room area, with two couches on either side, and a coffee table in between them. An old, ratty easy chair sat off to the far side of the couch. Lining the far wall completely was a bookshelf crammed with novels, reference books, and board games.

Beyond the living room was a kitchenette. It had a sink and a single electric burner and closed wood cabinets.

17 MILES

It was hard to see beyond that but I was pretty sure there were bunks back there for sleeping.

I put my hand on the wall – cold metal. The whole bunker was made out of steel, though some of the furniture was wood.

Batiste and then Ulysses stepped in behind us.

'Praise the Lord,' Batiste whispered and I fully agreed.

Suddenly a machine came roaring to life and there was a strong sucking sound near our feet. Everyone jumped.

'What is it?' Batiste asked me.

I sniffed. The air tasted weird. Like ozone.

I reached down and felt a long, thin vent at ground level. It was sucking in the air.

'It's an air-filtration system,' I guessed. 'It must come on automatically when it senses impurities in the air.'

Batiste and Ulysses lay down on the two couches. Niko struggled down with Max in his arms.

'You two get off the couches,' Mario ordered. Batiste and Ulysses slunk onto the floor.

'Put the hurt boy there,' Mario ordered Niko.

Mario unzipped his coveralls, removed them, and bundled them into a rubberized stuff sack. He did it pretty quickly, for an old guy.

'Gotta think here. Gotta think about what to do first,' he muttered.

He went past the kitchen to a closet set in the wall.

'What can I do?' Niko said. He was standing, hunched over, near the couches, and looked about a million years old.

'Get his boots off if you can.'

Niko started to tug at Max's boots and Max let out a shrieking howl.

'All right, all right, just let him be for a moment,' Mario said, tottering in with two of those plastic caddies people sometimes use to carry around cleaning stuff. You know the kind I mean. These two were filled with medical supplies. Mario put his hand on the couch and lowered himself down to sitting so he was perched next to Max.

'Okay, should be okay now. You kids take off your layers. They're loaded with compounds.'

'You.' He pointed to Sahalia. 'There are trash bags under the counter. Get one and collect all the clothing.'

Sahalia groaned, but got onto her hands and knees and crawled over to the kitchen.

The rest of us, I guess we didn't move fast enough for him.

'Get on there! Take off your layers! You can't be *that* tired, now!'

He was wrong. We were more tired than it's possible even to be. We were completely wrung out, each one of us.

We started to peel off the layers, moving as slow as zombies.

'You kids need to hurry! The air filter's automatic. It'll keep sucking until you guys are clean. And that's not going to happen with those filthy outfits on.'

Mario went over to Ulysses and started pulling his sweatshirt off.

'I don't think you understand. The air filter's automatic. It'll keep running until all our solar is used up. Then it'll start in on the gas generator. I only have a couple days' worth of gas. So you kids gotta hop to and get these layers off and closed up in a bag.'

Ulysses started to cry. Mario was scaring him.

17 MILES

Ulysses had the outline of his face mask etched in red around his face. His tears spilled down his dirty face.

'Oh, for God's sake. Don't cry,' Mario said, his voice softening a little. He let go of Ulysses's sleeve. 'We'll get you cleaned up, son. Just get these clothes off.'

As the layers came off, we became the shape of little kids again.

There was Batiste, his straight black hair matted to his head.

Ulysses's pot belly hanging out from under his monster truck T-shirt. The T-shirt had something dribbled down the front. Vomit, I think.

Niko took off his layers and got thinner and thinner. Was he so thin before? He looked like a skeleton. He looked tiny. I had remembered him as being so big and grown-up. Now he looked just like a sick teenage boy.

It was weird, taking off the layers. They felt like a part of me. I felt sort of naked without them.

But in the end I was just wearing the navy-blue long johns that were my base layer.

I remembered picking them out back at Greenway. I'd felt so hopeful then.

Dean, if you ever read this, you were right. If I'd known what would happen, how horrible and difficult it would turn out to be, and that Brayden would die anyway, and that Josie would go wild and run away and leave us, I never would have supported Niko's decision to go.

Was it so stupid to think we could get to Denver? I guess so.

What do we know? We're just stupid kids.

Sahalia took off her last sweatshirt and the whole T-shirt came

170

off, like sometimes happens. I saw her boobs in her lacy bra. Big whoop.

We threw the clothes on the floor and Sahalia gathered them up. She put them in the garbage bag. Then she got out another one for our boots and masks.

Mario had Max's mask off and was opening a little foil pack of pills.

I didn't like what I saw. Max's face was mottled with blisters. Around his mouth they were the worst. It looked like he'd had some kind of bike accident. Like he'd skidded across the pavement on his face. His eyes were screwed shut and he was stifling his cries.

Mario carefully opened up Max's lips and teeth and placed a pill in his mouth.

Almost instantly, Max's expression softened and his body went limp.

'Gave him some powerful stuff. But should be enough for us to get him cleaned up.'

'Do you have Benadryl?' Niko asked. 'It's worked for us in the past.'

Then Niko staggered backward and just caught himself before he fell. He struggled to stand. He was on his feet, but barely.

'Sit down,' Mario snapped. 'You fall on me and you'll crush me.'

Niko collapsed onto the easy chair.

'That's my chair,' Mario growled. Then he took a second look at Niko and changed his tone. 'But you can stay there for a bit.'

Mario fished a pack of pills out of his caddy and tossed it in Niko's lap.

'Benadryl. Take four.' He looked around and his eyes caught

17 MILES

mine. 'You, there. Can you get your friend a glass of water?'

'Okay,' I said.

'Glasses in first cabinet there and water's in the corner. Not too much water at first, you kids. Take two sips, then wait a moment. Then two more and so on. Otherwise you'll all retch.'

I opened the shelves. It seemed like it had been years since I opened a kitchen cabinet and looked at stacks of dishes and glasses standing neatly in a line.

I took a jelly glass from the shelf. It had cherries painted on it and a yellow stripe around the rim.

Against the wall there was a large spring water bottle on a stand.

'Can I have some water, too?' Sahalia asked. 'Please?'

Her voice was funny and I saw she was crying.

'Of course. You all need water right away. And food, too. We'll get to that. First I have to help this one. And you have to get cleaned up.'

My hand shook as I filled the jelly glass. I took two sips.

It was so clean, that water. I felt it go into my chest and through my whole, parched body, it felt like.

Sahalia had come next to me and I gave her the glass. She took a long drink.

'Can we have some too?' Batiste asked.

I went over to him and let him drink from the glass. Then Ulysses had some and by that time there was none left for Niko.

'There are enough glasses for everyone, you kids,' Mario crabbed.

But we were used to sharing. We didn't care.

I refilled the glass and took two more sips. Then I walked over and gave it to Niko. His hands were bloody and blistered.

'Thanks,' he said. His voice like gravel.

'Fella, what's your name?' Mario asked me.

'Alex Grieder,' I told him.

'Well, I'm Mario Scietto. You seem to have your wits about you. You want to help me with this one?' He nodded toward Max.

'Max,' I supplied. 'Sure.'

'You, missy!' Mario said to Sahalia. 'There's a shower in the back.'

'Oh my God, really?' Sahalia asked, perking up.

'It's on a timer. You can each have two minutes. Hot water and everything, but two minutes is all, you hear me? It's well water, and it's a good deep well, but the hot water heater takes too much power.'

'Yes, sir.'

'And be smart about it. Use soap and shampoo and scrub 'til you're clean. Don't waste water – it's the only shower you're going to get.'

'Yes, sir.'

'And put your underthings in a bag, too. The lot of you stink to high heaven. Put those boys in first and watch over them. When they get out, there's clean clothes you'll find in the dresser back there. Put them in some of my pajamas, you hear. And there's some women's clothes you can use, for yourself.'

'Come on, you guys,' Sahalia said, herding Batiste and Ulysses to their feet.

No arguments from them – they went off to the back, stumbling with tiredness, but excited to get clean.

I glanced at Niko. He was already asleep.

'Now, we're going to remove your friend's layers and then we're

17 MILES

going to clean and treat his wounds,' Mario said. 'Do you think you can help me to do that?'

I nodded.

'Good boy.'

I almost fell asleep a couple times, but I helped Mario bathe and bandage Max's feet.

There was some Troxoidal in one of the caddies. I remembered it as the demi-steroid Jake had been handing out to speed healing.

'This might help him,' I said, showing Mario the pack.

I said it like a fact, but it was more of a question.

'Good thinking,' Mario told me, examining the pack. 'Adult dosage is two tabs every six hours. Let's give him half that.'

So I popped out a pill and put it under Max's tongue. It melted almost right away. It was still a little bloody in there, in the spit.

Sahalia, Batiste, and Ulysses had all showered by the time we got Max's feet wrapped up.

'Wish I had a bathtub,' Mario muttered as he finished wrapping Max's feet in gauze.

'Why?' I asked.

'Well, I still gotta get Max here clean. He's going to trigger the air filter with all this filth.'

He lifted the seat of the couch opposite us. The whole couch had a storage space under the seat.

Pretty cool. I guess in a bomb shelter every inch counts.

The storage space was filled with blankets. He took out a metallic blanket. Like the one that Niko brought you, Dean, back at Greenway after the hailstorm. Do you remember?

He wrapped the blanket over Max.

'Maybe that'll help,' he said to himself. Then he tucked one over Niko's sleeping body for good measure.

I got the feeling that he cared more about getting the air filter to turn off than he did about their warmth, but I didn't begrudge him that.

'I could take a look at your air-filtration system,' I offered. 'I'm good with power systems.'

'Nope, I don't want you poking around back there.' He glanced at a metal door at the end of the bunker. It probably led to a machine room of some kind.

Then my stomach growled. Really loud.

'What's that you say?' Mario asked.

'I didn't say anything.'

'Yeah, you did.'

'No, it was just—'

My stomach made another sound.

'You're growling at me. What kind of thing is that to do, after all I done for you?'

I looked at him. Was he serious? Was Mario actually mad at me?

No, he was joking. His eyes were twinkling. He gave my knee a slap.

I tend to read machines better than I read people.

'Go hop in the shower. While you clean up, I'll get some food ready.'

It was a feast. To us, anyway.

Lentil soup, brown rice, graham crackers, and applesauce.

Batiste and Ulysses were both in Mario's pajamas. Sahalia was

17 MILES

wearing some kind of baggy dress she'd found in the bunkroom. She made it look cool, somehow.

I had on a white T-shirt and a pair of grey sweatpants.

We all sat around the table (the table was just beyond the kitchen, but before the bunkroom) and grinned at one another.

Mario busied himself fussing in the kitchen and both telling us not to eat too fast and also to eat more at the same time.

We kept offering Mario some soup, but he waved us away.

'I hate that lentil soup,' he grouched. 'I'm glad to give it to you. Now, I won't have to eat it.'

'More, please,' Ulysses said, holding out his bowl.

Mario ruffled Ulysses's hair.

He could be nice, when he wasn't barking out orders or yelling at us about hot water.

Just as we finished eating, Niko woke up.

Mario sent him right to the shower.

While Niko was in the shower, Mario decided we needed to get Max clean, too. Mario and I stripped Max down to his undies, which was weird since Max was totally konked out. But he really did need to get clean. He had so many blisters and open sores – I knew he was at risk of infection.

Sahalia helped me to carry Max to the shower where we basically handed him to Niko, who was just rinsing off.

Niko held Max while I lathered him up.

Mario had taped plastic Baggies over Max's bandaged feet, but blood from his face and his other blisters went swirling down the drain along with grit and general filth. I had had plenty of that, too, during my shower.

Eventually the water went clear, though it did take longer than two minutes. Mario looked the other way on that one.

'Lay him down on the last bunk,' Mario directed when the shower was done. He had sealed Niko's and Max's clothes in a bag

Niko walked out of the shower wet and completely naked and lay Max in the bunk.

I admire Niko. Sometimes I don't know how he does it. He didn't seem to care at all that Sahalia could see his naked everything. I would have rather died.

The air filter, finally, turned off.

'That's a relief,' Mario said.

The bunks were long and narrow. We could fit two kids on each, toe to toe. Sahalia took the first one with Ulysses at her feet. I took the one above them.

I got into bed and it felt like heaven. To be safe and warm again was the best feeling in the world.

Mario came over and tucked me in. It was cute. And I kind of liked it.

'Mr Scietto?' I asked quietly.

'Yes?'

'Do we really have to leave tomorrow? I just wanted to know.'

'We'll see, Alex. I don't know. It depends on the power system.'

'If we could stay for a couple more days, I know Max would get better . . .'

Mario did that corny old bit where he pretended to grab my nose.

'You're a good boy. You follow directions and you're polite,' he said. 'Maybe you should think about staying with me. I have enough provisions for two, to last us near seven weeks, if we're careful. I

17 MILES

rather think the mess upstairs will be sorted by then.'

It was nice, to be asked. I said I would think about it.

But I didn't really think about it. I mean, I did like the idea of working on his system. And I didn't want to go back into the violent, horrible world above.

But I didn't really think about it. Not for very long, anyway.

19 ALEX

I TOTALLY BLEW IT. I blew it for us.

The air filter came on. That's all.

It was the middle of the night and everyone was asleep and I knew Mario would be upset it was on again, so I just thought I would take a look at the system. I figured there had to be a way to shut it off manually.

I went quietly to the door to the machine room and it came right open.

Then I heard Mario's voice say, 'Stop! No!'

But it was too late.

I saw what was inside.

Now he's packing things. I can hear him in the dark, muttering to himself and cursing. He's bustling all around, opening drawers. A little while ago he was back here in the bunk area, taking clothes out of a drawer.

17–10 MILES

He would have let us stay for a few more days, I just know it.

He would have let us stay until Max could walk again.

But I had to go looking in the machine room. And I saw her body there.

All wrapped up like a mummy.

His wife. It had to be.

The shape of a body is the shape of a body. You cannot pretend you didn't see it or that you do not recognize it for what it is. Even if you really, really want to.

Mario scurried over and shut the door.

'Nosy, nosy, nosy!' he whispered. 'You had to go poking around!'

'What's going on?' came Niko's voice, instantly alert.

'What's wrong?' said Sahalia.

'Nothing,' I said softly. 'I just opened the wrong door. Everyone go back to sleep.'

They were quiet after a moment.

Mario gestured for me to follow him into the kitchen. He glared at me for a long moment. I noticed he was trembling.

Then he whispered, 'I built this place for us to share, me and Judy. I wasn't going to stay here without her. She couldn't make me promise and I won't do it!'

I tried to talk to him, to make him understand that I wouldn't tell about . . . Judy.

But he just pointed toward my bunk.

In the morning I saw he'd laid out all this stuff for us to take with us. A set of clothes for each kid. Three new backpacks that were loaded with water and these protein shakes you can drink with a built-in straw so Max and Niko can even drink them on the road.

And he'd cleaned our boots and masks.

He does care about us, but he's making us leave.

Niko took the news very well.

He just nodded and said, 'You gave us more than you said you would and we're thankful.'

While we all got ready, I saw Niko hand Mario a letter. I couldn't hear what they were saying, but I bet the letter is for Josie. I don't know how Niko thinks that Mario would come across Josie. Chances are better that she'd find us on the road. But, I guess it can't hurt to be prepared.

After Mario showed Niko all the stuff he was giving us, Niko thanked him again.

'Do you have any rope?' Niko asked him.

'What for?' Mario asked.

'I want to figure out a way to rig up a carrier of some kind for Max. I thought I could tie him, somehow, to my back.'

At this, Mario got quiet.

'Well, I was thinking . . . maybe Max should stay here with me.'

It took us a moment for his words to soak in and then there was a group recoil, like he'd puked or something. Ulysses cried out and Batiste shrieked no and Sahalia started yelling her head off.

'I know you don't want to leave him.' Mario tried to speak over the loud protests but it was no good. 'SIMMER DOWN!' he shouted. 'I know you all don't like the idea, but maybe Max would like to stay. Why don't we ask him?'

From the back, Max shouted weakly, 'Not a chance in hell.'

So Mario Scietto finally came to understand that we were not a group you could divide.

We walked.

It was better than before. For one thing, the road was pretty flat and straight. Also, we were rested, well fed, and had new clothes. Old boots but new clothes.

Mario had told Niko which houses in the development might have a pushchair. Niko had found a good pushchair, too. A jogging pushchair. If Max felt embarrassed to be pushed along like a baby, he didn't mention it. He was all wrapped up in a blue-and-orange Denver Broncos rain poncho Mario had given us.

We were walking on a road called Gun Club Road, which seemed sort of ominous, but the area there is flat and blah. Just mile after mile of nothing. No houses or buildings or rest stops.

Of course, there still were cars on and around the highway and cars were scary. Someone could be hiding in them, so we had to approach each one carefully. But mostly they were molded over and everything was quiet. It was deserted.

Gun Club Road runs fairly close to 470, so when we'd get close to the highway we would see some clusters of cars on the edge, but that was fine.

We walked and walked and walked. At first, I had thoughts in my head, but then the *trudge*, *trudge*, *trudge* of my feet on the road was so rhythmic, my brain stopped its spinning.

All there was was one foot in front of the other.

We might live. We might die. But it seemed like we'd never stop walking.

* * *

After many hours, Ulysses asked Niko to tell a Mrs Wooly story.

'I can't,' Niko said.

'Why not?' Max asked.

'It makes me too sad.'

'I know why,' Batiste said, huffing a little from our pace. 'You think she's dead.'

'No!' Ulysses protested. 'Mrs Wooly?'

'Please, Niko, please? I'm so tired,' Max complained.

'What are you tired from?' I snapped. 'You're getting pushed in a pushchair!'

'Aargh. Okay, everyone, be quiet!' Niko said. His voice sounded cold coming through the transmitter in the air mask.

'Mrs Wooly's going to come down this road we're on,' he said.

'What will she be driving?' Max asked.

'A van.'

'What kind of van?'

'Oh my God . . . She'll be driving a . . . a Kia Sportvan.'

'Red?' asked Max. 'With a sunroof?'

'Red, with a sunroof. And she'll say, 'I was just going to get you at Mr Scietto's house. I knew he was taking care of you there while I got this van.' '

'How'd she get the van, anyway?' Max asked.

'Well, that's the reason she's taken so long.'

'What do you mean?' Batiste asked.

'She had to earn the money to buy the van.'

'What's she been doing, then?' Max asked.

'I don't know,' Niko said.

He had to push the pushchair up over a little hill and the soggy ground was giving him trouble.

'Maybe she's been stealing it from people,' Max said.

'Or maybe she dug a pit and trapped some people,' Batiste added.

'Ugh, never mind,' Niko snapped.

There was quiet for a while.

And I just thought, step, step, step.

'How much farther?' Batiste or Max or Ulysss would ask.

'A while,' Niko would answer.

That happened about 20 times.

Step, step, step.

Ulysses started crying softly.

It wasn't a cry like he was asking for attention. Just pure misery.

And suddenly Sahalia's voice rang out.

She has a good voice, kind of high and gravelly, like a punk-rock girl.

I think it was a rock song, but it was a little hard to tell, just her voice alone on the wind.

These were the words:

Well, now I sat
on the floor of that pub.
That dirty floor
is where I sat.

And my old friend
came to my side.
And he knelt down

where I was at.

She's gone and left,
I cried out loud.
I guess I'm just
a hopeless case.

And so my friend,
he cursed her name.
And then he slapped
me on the face.

He said: Get up, get up, get up, m'boy.
Get up now, lad, get up!
She's gone for good, I heard you say.
But you'll not die today, today.
No, you'll not die today.

He walked me out,
onto the street.
The icy air,
it burned my throat.

I said let me grieve.
He laughed at that.
Then he grabbed
me by the coat.

And he proclaimed:

The pain is good,
the pain will burn
and make you strong.

But needless sufferin',
that's for the weak.
And then he made
me sing his song.

I said: Get up, get up, get up. I will!
Get up now, I'll get up!
She's gone for good, I'm sad to say.
But I'll not die today, today.
No, I'll not die today.

She repeated the chorus and I sang with her and so did a couple of the others. We sang softly so our voices didn't carry very far in the black air – I don't think.

It was a catchy song. Kind of uplifting, and at the same time sad.

Sahalia seemed to have a talent for picking the right songs for the right moments. That's something I could never do.

I thought about that for a while as we walked. I thought about Sahalia. She had changed a lot since I had known her. A lot of change, it seemed to me, in a short amount of time. Maybe I had changed, too. That was certainly possible. But I liked this Sahalia much better than I had liked the old one.

'How much farther?' Max or Batiste or Ulysses would still ask every so often.

'A while,' Niko would still say.

After that happened, like, maybe 50 more times, Sahalia hissed, 'Niko.'

'What?' he said.

'Behind us,' she whispered.

There was a little dot of light behind us. Maybe a quarter mile away.

Someone else was on the road.

'Keep an eye on them, okay?' Niko asked.

But then, maybe 10 minutes later, we saw another group of travellers ahead of us. They came off the highway and down to our road.

They had 3 flashlights and were shining them all around. Not very inconspicuous. Kind of stupid.

But they seemed to be moving quickly and soon they were quite a ways ahead of us.

'Who are they?' Max whispered.

'They're travellers,' Niko answered. 'Just like us.'

I looked at Sahalia and we smiled.

'They're trying to get to the airport. Just like us,' Niko repeated.

I cannot say how far we walked, that last march. If we had been closer to the highway, I could have calculated it with the mile markers. I imagine we could walk a mile in 30–40 minutes.

When we left Mario's, it was 8:32 a.m. We stopped for protein shakes and water at 11:15. Then we walked again until 1:30.

Maybe 5 miles?

Well, let's say 5 miles +/- 2 miles from Mario's we saw a light in the distance. Much brighter than the emergency lights on the side of the highway. This one was shining in a circle, spinning its head around, like a lighthouse light.

It was a beacon.

'What is that?' Max asked. 'Are we there? Is that the airport? Are we there?'

'I don't know,' Niko said.

We picked up the pace.

Sahalia smiled at me. A big, real smile.

Batiste squeezed my hand.

We could hear a man's voice on a loudspeaker. We couldn't make out the words, but you could hear that it was some kind of a message, because the cadence repeated.

As we drew closer, we saw people gathered around the light. They stood a ways apart from one another, in small groups. Some groups were just couples and some groups had as many as 8–10 people. Most of them wore layers and face masks. There were a few people raving and acting dodgy – they must have been type AB.

We made our way up to the group. Slowly, edging forward. Niko had Sahalia push Max. I guess he wanted his hands free in case we needed to fight. He was probably wishing he still had our gun, but I didn't say anything.

No one moved towards us or anything.

The other people looked as ragged and filthy as we had before Mario's. We definitely looked the best out of everyone. Relatively clean, with the two cool orange Army face masks (no one else had those).

I felt like if Mario could have seen us, he would have been proud.

The message came on again: 'You have reached an assembly

point for the emergency evacuation of the Four Points area. Remain here until the next bus arrives. Buses will arrive every hour on the hour.'

I was so dazed, hearing that.

We had made it.

Sahalia let out a big whoop of joy. She hugged me and kissed me right on the mouth!

Ulysses went to Max and hugged him and they cried together, and Batiste was hugging me from behind as Sahalia, now with her arm draped around my shoulders, gave another big whoop!

The other people joined in with her. Maybe it took her elation to set them off, but suddenly everyone was laughing, crying, hugging one another, where before Sahalia had made that sound, they were reserved and defensive.

And then I saw Niko. He had sunk down to his knees and had his face his hands.

I went over to him.

'You did it,' I said. 'You saved us.'

'Yeah,' he moaned. 'But I lost her.'

The bus came, just like it said it would, on the hour. Okay, it was 12 minutes late but who cared!

It was a school bus. But painted Army green.

The door opened up and the driver (not Mrs Wooly, of course not) was a soldier wearing an Army air mask.

'Welcome aboard,' he said with his metallic-sounding voice. 'We'll have you safe and inside in no time.'

We filed onto the bus. Somehow Sahalia had broken the ice and the people from the different groups were starting to talk to one another.

A man with a beard asked me where we were from. When I said Monument, he couldn't believe it.

'That's over 60 miles away!' he exclaimed. 'We had a hell of a time and we're just from Castle Rock.'

I shrugged. But I was happy inside.

'How'd you do it?' he asked.

'It was Niko,' I said. I pointed to Niko, who had Max on his lap in the seat across from me.

'No,' interrupted Batiste, who was sitting with me. 'It was God.'

The bus went so fast, Dean! The road was entirely cleared. We were in a military zone now and everything was different.

When we passed through the places with big stores and office buildings, it looked like there had been a war. There was bullet spray on the walls, and burned out Jeeps and some of the buildings were on fire.

I saw bodies stacked into a great, long pile. For burial, I hope, not burning. Though I guess at this point, nobody cared.

The closer we got to the airport, the more cars there were. All the fields around the airport were just filled with cars. Cars parked at crazy angles, not like a tidy parking lot, but like a jigsaw puzzle. Crammed in every which way.

Large drifts of the white moss-mold enveloped the cars in places. The moss grew in waves, up and down, ebbing and flowing through the cars. It looked like an art installation, actually. An ocean of car bodies and mold.

And there was Denver International Airport, its white peaks lit up from inside. Rising up out of the car field like a castle.

Everybody cheered. Well, not everybody. There were people like Niko who seemed terribly sad or deeply in shock. But Sahalia and the kids and I cheered and many other people joined in.

We pulled up to a set of glass double doors. We had made it, Dean. We made it to DIA.

17-10 MILES

20 DEAN

I WOKE UP ON A satiny bedspread on the floor.

Around me came the snores of the other cadets.

I tried to sit up and my body protested plenty, but the screaming, brain-hole-drilling shoulder pain of the day before was gone.

I couldn't figure out what time it was. Was it morning? Night?

From across the space there was a light shining. I squinted. It was Kildow, I thought. He seemed to be reading something.

I closed my eyes, just to rest them for a second.

And then I was being nudged awake by a boot.

Payton looked down at me. He carried a mug of water and was brushing his teeth.

'How's the shoulder, Deano?'

'Better,' I said.

'Better, sir!'

'Better, sir!' I repeated. I groaned, sitting up. But it *was* better.

The cadets were eating Pop-Tarts and drinking iced teas for breakfast.

'Show us where the batteries and lights are. We want to get a little more light going. Don't they have any generators in here? You know, like those portable ones?'

'Not that we've found,' I said.

I could lead them to the aisle with the lights but they'd see that all the Christmas lights and the lanterns were missing. Aargh.

'I thought I saw a generator,' Jake said.

'No,' I answered. 'We don't have any.'

'Yeah, near the leaf blowers and stuff.'

'What are you talking about?'

'Ladies, ladies, figure it out,' Payton said. 'We're doing physical conditioning in thirty and I want as much light as possible. Then we do a total inventory on this place. I want it listed down to the tampon.'

'Sir, yes, sir!' shouted Jake.

'Sir, yes, sir!' I echoed, late and sounding lame.

'Dismissed, doolies,' Payton said with a fond chuckle.

Jake led me toward Home Improvement.

'Why did you say we have a generator?' I hissed as soon as we were out of earshot. 'They're gonna be disappointed!'

DAY 15

'I was just trying to get you alone for a second,' he answered. 'Look, we're going to have to kill them . . . It's the only way to keep Astrid and the kids safe.'

'We can't kill five guys, Jake,' I protested.

'We just need to get that semiautomatic from the black kid.'

'I don't want to kill five guys, Jake! You don't know what it's like!'

Jake gave me a hard look.

'They killed Brayden. My best friend. They *killed* him! You think we should just forget about that?' Jake snapped.

'Jake, you're not thinking clearly,' I protested.

'They killed him and I'm going to make them pay.'

'It won't make you feel better,' I said.

'No, I know that. Nothing will ever make me feel better,' he said. He shrugged his shoulders. 'But we have to keep Astrid safe. So we're going to kill those cadets.'

'No, Jake,' I said. 'We just need to get our hands on Anna. We get her as a hostage, maybe we can make them leave!'

Jake looked at me, chewing the side of his mouth.

'All right. Shoot. Yeah, that's a better plan,' he said.

'Hey!' Zarember came at a run. 'Don't make Payton wait! That's the first thing you need to know!'

In the space where the bus had sat, Payton had had his cadets make a little gym.

They had brought over the weights from the Sports

aisle, and they had laid down a bunch of rubber mats – the kind you lock together.

Jake had snatched some of the battery-powered lanterns from the House.

We should have just told them about it at the beginning. It was like a time bomb – when Payton found that House hidden away, he was going to lose it.

Jake set up the lanterns and I brought some car batteries and clip-on desk lamps in their boxes. I told Payton I thought there must be a way to jerry-rig them to the car batteries.

'Now there's some resourcefulness. Look at that!' Payton commanded the cadets.

'Thank you, sir!' I yelled.

Every time I did that I felt like a phony and a fraud.

Because of my arm, my 'gimpy arm' as Payton put it, I was excused from physical conditioning.

I worked on getting the lights set up while Payton put Jake and the others through a gruelling routine of weight lifting and cardio.

'That's it, Simonsen!' he hollered. 'Get under it. Come on, Zarember, push, push, push!'

Jake actually seemed to be enjoying it.

I saw Anna drifting toward the Girls' clothing section.

I put the light down.

I would follow her into the aisle and I would grab her.

The thought made me sick to my stomach.

But to save Astrid?

I could do it.

DAY 15

'Where you going?' Payton demanded.

'No-nowhere,' I stammered.

Payton crossed to me in three strides. He grabbed me by the shirtfront.

'Anna's off-limits, you hear me? No one touches her. No one thinks about her. Got that?' He got up so close that spit from his mouth sprayed me in the face. His teeth were yellow and his breath minty fresh.

'Yes,' I said. 'Yes, sir!'

'I tell you what, you have so much time on your hands, why don't you make us some lunch?!'

What is it about me that screams 'cook'?

I went to the Food aisles, in the exact opposite direction of where Anna had headed.

What could I make these idiots? And what could I cook over a brass fire pit?

Soup, I decided. Chunky soup – the kind with those little hamburgers in it. Payton would like that.

We had some saltines, too.

I didn't even hear her coming.

She touched me on the shoulder and I turned and Astrid was in my arms, kissing me hard, holding me to her.

'Where are you hiding?' I whispered when our kiss ended. 'It's not safe.'

Astrid pointed up.

'I just . . . I had to give you these.'

She pressed three foil packs into my hand. The sleeping pills. The EZ-melt ones. The ones that had knocked Chloe out for a day and a half.

'We used one on Luna and I thought . . .'

Of course. Sleeping pills.

'It's brilliant,' I said. 'Now go.'

She took my hand and led me to the next aisle and I saw the tile ajar in the ceiling.

I could see Caroline and Henry and Chloe peeking out. They looked tired and scared and grimy.

Caroline gave a little wave.

Astrid brought her face close to my ear and whispered, 'Look, I want you to know that you're - you're the one for me. In case we die. I want you to know.'

And as lightly as a cat, she climbed back up the shelves and up into her nest in the ceiling.

I rushed into the next aisle.

I had to get the pills into something. And fast. But not the soup. It would be hot and, no, they might not all eat it.

Juice.

There it was.

That kind with the carrots and vegetables in it. Yes, yes, yes.

It was sweet, really sweet, but had veggies so if it tasted a little off . . .

I grabbed two large bottles and took them to the back of the aisle.

I hoped that if someone came looking for me, I'd have time to hide the pills.

197

DAY 15

I unscrewed the tops off the two bottles and started pressing the sleeping pills out of the packs. There were eight pills in each pack and I had three packs. Well, two pills were out of one of the packs but it was still a lot of pills.

My heart hammered in my chest as I popped the pills into the juice.

Twenty-two sleeping pills. Eleven in each bottle.

Twenty-two sleeping pills to fell five cadets and to save our lives.

21 ALEX

IT'S HARD TO DESCRIBE how huge the operation at the airport was.

First, we went into a waiting area for all new arrivals. There were about 200 other people when we got there, and every 10 minutes or so, another busload would arrive, adding 5–20 people.

They had taken seats from the airport gates and put them in there. They weren't bolted to the floor so they wobbled, but they'd basically made a big waiting area.

Everywhere there were signs: EVERYONE MUST WEAR A MASK AT ALL TIMES.

There were air masks piled on the tables. Some were used, some were new.

There weren't any Army ones, like our two, available, but there was a different kind, like an Army-issue mask for civilians. I found one for me, and for Sahalia and Batiste. I put mine on and there

10–0 MILES

was a distinct smell of some kind of fruit. I hated that smell but I couldn't remember what fruit it was.

'Ugh,' Sahalia groaned. 'Why do we need these? The damage has been done, for God's sake.'

But we wore them. Everyone did. Because if you didn't, an Army guy with a rifle would come over and shove one into your hands.

I think that they made us wear them for the sake of the type ABs. Obviously the type Os and As knew to keep their masks on.

But I had seen some ABs, paranoid and wild-eyed, on the bus. I guess some ABs were functional enough to get themselves to safety, but not rational enough to keep a mask on. With a mask on, those same crazy people looked sedate. Exhausted and worn-out, but sedate.

It was an unreasonable assumption for me to make, but in some part of my brain, I thought that as soon as we got to DIA, I would find our parents. Like they'd be waiting right by the door or something.

But I scanned every masked face in that waiting room. Each of us did, except Max, who was asleep in his pushchair.

'They're not here,' Batiste said, voicing exactly what I'd been thinking.

'I know,' I said. 'But maybe inside. Maybe inside . . .'

Our little group all sat together in some chairs.

A team of soldiers in hazmat suits with, get this, *pads and paper* came around and wrote down our names, addresses, and social security numbers, if we knew them.

'Is there some kind of list?' I asked the man who took my information. 'Of the survivors? Of the people who are here now?'

'We're putting it together, kid,' he said. I couldn't really see his face, but he sounded tired.

He put a bracelet on my wrist. It had a number. He wrote the number down on the pad, next to my name, and also had an old-fashioned handheld scanner, which he used to scan the barcode on my bracelet.

That was good. I was in the system now. All of us were. That would help our parents find us, it had to.

'The Network still down?' I asked him.

He held up the yellow pad. 'What do you think?'

He was ready to move on, but I put a hand on his arm. He pulled it away.

'My brother and four other kids are stranded back at the Greenway in Monument,' I told him. 'We need to organize a rescue.'

He snorted.

'You can write a request,' he said. 'But the chances are slim.'

'Why?' I asked.

'We're spread real thin, in case you hadn't noticed.'

'But they can't come out because they're O. And they're kids. They need help.'

He leaned down and put his mask right up against mine.

He had brown skin and dark eyes. A kind face, but a tired one.

'You know how many refugees have come through here?' he asked me. 'Me neither. Nobody does. We've lost track. But more than eight hundred thousand. Eight hundred thousand people, kid. We can hardly take care of the people we have here. We don't need to go getting any more.'

10-0 MILES

When he said those things to me, I cried. I knew he was right and I knew we'd never get anyone to go back for you.

I cried then, good and long. Sahalia held me like I was a little kid, and I didn't even care.

We wouldn't be able to go back for you, Dean.

Every 45 minutes, a soldier would come and shout out a bunch of numbers.

People would look at their bracelet, to see if it was their number being called. Then the ones called would stand up and take all their stuff, and go to the big double doors.

It was always 30 males and 30 females. We had been told we'd all be decontaminated in a big group shower and then given new clothes and gear.

After we waited for a while, it was our turn.

We all stood up and went over to the door, with the other people whose numbers had been listed.

Sahalia took my hand and held on to it tight.

Niko pushed Max in his pushchair. He looked scared.

They had 2 soldiers (in hazmat suits) checking names off a shared master (paper) list.

When it got to us, they stopped Niko.

'That kid needs to go to medical,' one said, pointing to Max. But we'd seen people getting taken away to medical. They were separated from their families and had to go alone. Max had outright refused.

'He's okay,' Niko said. 'I can take care of him.'

'Suit yourself,' answered the soldier.

Niko picked Max up and carried him in, leaving the bloody,

mucky pushchair to the side.

We were now in a weird, flexible hallway. It was tall and oval shaped – like we were in a vacuum cleaner hose. Airtight, obviously. It was big, too – 3 people could easily walk side by side in it.

A little ways down, the hallway branched in two and the men/ boys and women/girls were being separated.

Sahalia started to panic.

'Don't worry,' I told her. 'We'll find you on the other side.'

'Promise?'

'Promise.'

'Really?' she said, and her fingers clutched onto my jacket.

'We'll find you, Sahalia,' I vowed.

She nodded with tears in her eyes and went off with the women and girls.

We were herded into a big, big bubble room. It was shaped like a giant tangerine, and the things dividing the segments of the tangerine were flexible, white plastic pipes. There was a circle of them around the room and each came up to the centre of the bubble, where it hung down with a showerhead on the end of it.

Five large bins with lids stood in the corner, next to a stack of plastic stools.

Four more soldiers in hazmat suits were waiting for us.

A soldier set a plastic stool in front of Niko for Max to sit on. That was kind. He did the same for a couple of other people, who looked worse for wear.

'Leave your masks on,' one commanded us.

Would we ever get to take them off?

The soldier handed each of us a plastic Ziploc bag.

10-0 MILES

'Place any valuables and ID you have into this bag and put your name on it. You'll get it on the other side.'

I slipped my notebook, the digital watch I had taken from the Greenway, and my pen into the bag. I didn't have anything else worth saving. The soldier came and wrote my name on the bag for me and put it into a metal basket, along with all the other bags.

'Besides the masks, remove all your clothing and place it in these bins. All fabric *must* go in the bin to be destroyed. That's the policy,' the soldier dictated.

Some men started to protest but the lead soldier talked louder than them: 'On the other side of this room, there is a room filled with clothing and gear. You will have your pick of clean, new clothes on the other side. Everything you need will be provided for you. Now get to.'

Ulysses started crying. It was kind of scary. It was so white and bright, and now this guy was barking at us to get naked.

'It's okay, Ulysses,' Niko said calmly through his voice transmitter. 'We're going to be clean. It's good.'

Following Niko's example, we took off our clothes and threw them in the nearest bin. The men around us did the same.

That was a grisly collection of bodies, I tell you.

We were all just standing there, shivering in nothing but our face masks, when the lead soldier nodded to the other 3. They each picked up hoses from the floor. The hoses ran into the base of the walls. I hadn't noticed them before.

'This part's going to suck,' the lead soldier said. 'I apologize. Hit 'em!'

They turned on the hoses and jets of frothy orange wash came out of them. The four soldiers sprayed us all down.

There were shouts of protest and dismay.

Then the wash stopped.

'You can take off your masks now,' the soldier directed.

He gestured to a bin and we all tossed our masks inside.

Most of us had massive indentations on our faces from the masks. Everyone looked sort of googly-eyed and disoriented.

Then the lead soldier nodded again to the other 3 and they doused us with the foul cleanser again.

'This sucks!' shouted one man.

'I hate dis soap!' Ulysses shouted.

The lead soldier laughed. 'I know, kid. But it's the price of admission.'

He hit a large red button on a metal electrical box hanging on the wall.

Immediately hot water started pouring out of the showerheads and also spurting out from the pipes running down the walls.

It felt like heaven.

They gave us thin, scratchy towels to dry ourselves with and blue paper hospital outfits to wear. Like medical scrubs, but made of a waxy paper. I thought they were pretty cool, but there was some grumbling from the bigger men.

The soldiers led us out of the shower room and back into the hallway.

Niko had to carry Max. His feet were bleeding again and he looked pale and wiped out.

'Get that kid to medical, for God's sake,' the lead soldier said to Max.

'Yes, sir,' Niko answered.

10-0 MILES

We went down the hall and then came out into a large room.

A soldier in a uniform (no hazmat suit, no mask) greeted us.

'Breathe deeply, gentlemen, you're now in the safe zone. Welcome.'

Along the sides of the room were tables. They each had a sign of a size, like 'Men – Medium' or 'Boys 5T'. In the corner were a bunch of dressing rooms with curtains.

Behind each table were two civilians – two women, actually. The women were all different ages and dressed in all different ways but they all had something in common. It is hard to describe – at first I thought it was efficiency. Or maybe restlessness, like they had volunteered because if they didn't get to do something helpful they'd go crazy. Stressed and worn-out – but still hopeful.

That's when I realized what it was: They were moms.

It was like a department store run by moms.

And man, oh man, did they ever light up when they saw us kids.

A 40-something woman in a jogging suit just rushed right up to us. 'My poor, sweet darlings,' she said. She held out her arms and hugged Batiste and Ulysses. It seemed both totally inappropriate and totally perfect at the same time.

Another mom had me and was hugging me and praying in some Slavic language, I don't know which.

A black lady with red-dyed hair that was white at the temples came right out from behind a BOYS – 10–12 table. She just took Max from Niko and then pushed all the clothing and shoes off her table and set him down gently. She started barking orders to the others as she looked Max over: 'We need underwear and socks and sweatpants for this boy. Nothing binding, nothing uncomfortable. And thermals. Who has slippers? Nanette, bring slippers!'

The mothers swarmed over the rest of us. They brought us jeans and sweaters and sneakers. Everything new. They brought soft cotton underwear and socks with no seams. Only the best for us.

The men we'd come in with were left mostly to fend for themselves.

Then suddenly a loud, loud voice cut through everything.

'*Woo Sung-ah? Oori Woo Sung-ee maja? Woo Sung-ah!*'

And a short, Asian woman pushed through the crowd of moms.

'*Omma! Omma!*' Batiste was shouting and he reached for her. She was his mom.

He found his mom, Dean.

All that we went through, all the horrible things that happened to us. They were okay. They were for a reason because Batiste had found his mom.

She placed her palms on either side of his face and looked at him. Tears began to run down her face and she didn't even notice them. She just looked at the face of her boy.

Then she hugged him tight to her and she held him at arm's length again, looking into his face. It seemed like she was trying to drink in the sight of him.

'*Woo Sung-ah! Woo Sung-ah!*'

This was his name, I realized. His Korean name. Woo Sung-ah was our Batiste.

Then they started talking Korean, both at once.

Batiste, duh, is half Korean. I guess I knew that from the shape

10-0 MILES

of his face and his hair and everything, but he had no accent. I never thought he could speak Korean like that.

Everyone was hugging and laughing and crying. I mean, *all* the moms started crying and hugging us, and hugging each other and almost everybody was crying. It was a great moment.

Then Batiste's mom tried to take Batiste away from us. She wanted to squirrel him away, take him off to the rest of the family, I guess.

Batiste went rigid and refused, saying, '*An dwei-yo! Omoni.*'

He talked to her in his perfect, rapid-fire Korean, convincing her of something. She nodded.

He must have told her he wanted to introduce her to us.

Batiste said our names amid the Korean words. I heard 'Alex' and she glanced at me and nodded slightly. I bowed, which was a dorky thing to do and I immediately regretted it, but no one cared. Batiste went on to 'Ulysses' and Batiste's mom smiled at Ulysses. Max's face and feet got a critical look and she turned toward Batiste and gave him a mini harangue.

Batiste placated her, nodding and basically telling her, 'Yes, yes. We're going to get him taken care of right away.' I couldn't understand his words, but I could see what he was saying. Placating his mom and grinning all the while.

Then he introduced Niko. And she listened to what Batiste was saying. She was hearing, no doubt, that this worn-out-looking boy with serious brown eyes and the gaunt, haunted expression had saved the life of her son.

'*Niko-ya*...' she said, tears again in her eyes. '*Gompata. Nomu nomu gompata, Niko-ya.*'

She fumbled under her sweater and pulled a necklace over her head. It was a gold necklace, with a gold cross on it. A tiny Jesus there on the cross.

Batiste's mother pressed the necklace into Niko's palm and folded his fingers around it. Then she raised his hand and kissed the back of it again and again.

10-0 MILES

22 DEAN

I SCREWED THE TOPS ON tight and shook them. A little spilled on the top of one of the bottles. I wiped it on my T-shirt. They had to look *perfect*.

I set them in my cart along with the soup and the crackers. I raced over to the paper plate aisle and grabbed some of those blue keg cups.

When I came wheeling back toward the Kitchen, the boys were just finishing sets of frog jumps. They started from a squat and then had to jump up and touch their heels together and then land and do the whole thing again.

It looked hard as hell and the cadets, and Jake too, all looked like they might puke.

'Thirty seconds more! You can do it!'

I set up the juice on the table and chucked a Duraflame in the brass fire pit.

'Fifteen seconds, don't give up!'

I set the soup cans on the counter and grabbed a saucepan.

'Done! Good work, men!'

There were groans and curses from the cadets as they all basically collapsed.

'You guys should hydrate!' Payton commanded them.

Payton strolled over to me in the kitchen. He picked up one of the juice bottles and looked at it.

I tried not to stiffen.

'Drink water,' Payton directed over his shoulder. 'You gotta hydrate with pure water.'

He put the juice bottle down and my heart sank.

I'd put all the pills in those bottles.

Dear God, what if Payton didn't like juice?

Payton headed off to the Food aisles. Maybe to find plain water.

I cursed to myself. I should have saved some of the pills. Were there more? Maybe there were more in the Pharmacy . . .

But then Kildow and Greasy came over. Both were sweaty and thirsty, apparently.

Kildow opened the bottle and poured a keg cup full. He didn't notice that the seal on the bottle was already broken. Or if he did, he didn't care.

Greasy grabbed the other bottle and drank right from it.

DAY 15

'That's gross, man,' Kildow told him.

'Who cares?' Greasy answered. 'There's aisles full of this stuff.'

He looked at the bottle.

'Ew, what is this?'

'It's juice, but it's got, like, vegetables in it,' I said.

'*It's juice, but it's got, like, vegetables in it,*' Greasy parroted, mocking me.

I shrugged.

Zarember came forward, taking the other bottle. He poured a tumbler of it and drank.

'Tastes good to me,' he said, winking at me.

I felt bad, Zarember was definitely the nicest one. Here he was standing up for me and I had just drugged him.

Jake ambled over.

'What's this?'

I tried to tell him with my eyes, but he didn't see me. Too dark.

'Juice,' I said. 'That kind Chloe liked.' I was trying to tell him somehow that, I don't know, the juice had the sleeping pills Niko had given Chloe and then I realized he wasn't even there when that happened. He had been out on the road.

Jake picked up the container and chugged.

'Jake!' I shouted, before I could stop myself.

And the cadets all looked at me.

I tried to play it cool.

'He's gonna puke, he chugs it like that . . .'

And somehow I was right. Jake set the bottle down (now only half-full) and took two steps away and vomited all over the floor.

The cadets laughed and clapped one another on the back.

I felt like I was going to have a heart attack.

Payton came back hauling two gallon jugs of water.

'You idiots,' he scolded good-naturedly, 'I told you to hydrate with water.'

Payton set the water down next to Jake.

'Welcome to the Air Force, son! You earned your first curl hurl!'

Laughing, Payton picked up the bottle of juice from the counter and smelled it.

'Smells off,' he said.

Payton hadn't drunk any and neither had the tall, gangly cadet, Jimmy Doll Hands.

Then Anna came back.

'There's a room,' she announced, sounding as bored as she could possibly sound. 'There's a camp stove and bunks in the back. It was all hidden away.'

'What?' Payton asked.

'They hid it from us,' Anna said. 'And there's lots of clothes there and stuff.'

Payton strode across the Kitchen, to where I was stirring the soup.

He grabbed me by the hurt shoulder.

The pain seared through me and I cried out.

DAY 15

'A secret? We take you in, we hook you up, make you part of our squadron, and you're keeping *secrets* from us?'

He threw me down to the ground and my head hit the side of the fire pit. Sparks flew up in the air.

Payton marched over to Jake.

Just then, Kildow sat down, heavily, into a bench.

Payton grabbed Jake by the hair and dragged him to his feet.

'WHAT ELSE YOU NEED TO TELL ME, JAKEY?' he screamed.

'Payton, please!' Jake pleaded. 'I'm sorry!'

'You're sorry?'

'We meant to tell you but then it was too late!'

'Yeah it's too late!' Payton shouted. He punched Jake in the face. 'Hit me back! Hit me back, you lying sack, and then we'll see what happens!'

Jake was bleeding from the nose. His head hung down. He looked defeated.

'You won't hit me back because you know I will destroy you!'

Payton kicked Jake in the side and he fell to the ground. Jake didn't move. He was out.

Then there was a heavy THWOMP kind of a sound and Greasy had passed out.

Zarember groaned and fell to his knees and then face forward onto the floor.

'What the hell?' Payton hollered. 'What did you do to my men?'

He looked up, and looked at me.

'It-it-it must be the juice,' Jimmy stammered. 'You and me didn't have any!'

'Grab him!' Payton shouted.

I tried to get away, but Jimmy caught my leg and tripped me.

Payton snatched a handgun from a pile of the cadets' gear.

Then he grabbed me and slammed me down onto the top of one of the tables in the Pizza Shack.

It was the same table I'd hidden under with Astrid during the earthquake, one million years ago.

Payton pressed the gun into my eye socket.

'I should never have trusted you, Deano. You got the look of a freakin' intellectual about you, you know that? What'd you do to my boys and why'd you keep secrets from me?'

Then there came two delicious sounds.

First a scream – 'Uncle *Payton*!' – from Anna.

And then the ROAR of a battery-powered chainsaw.

Astrid stood in the middle of the fallen cadets out on the gym space. She held the chainsaw in one hand and in the other she had Anna by the hair. In the darkness behind her, I could see the little kids.

'You get away from Dean,' she commanded.

DAY 15

23 ALEX

'WHERE *WERE* YOU GUYS?!' Sahalia shouted. 'I've been waiting for an hour! I thought I'd lost you.'

She looked small and scared. I always thought of her as being so mature. But now she looked her age. The same age as me, that is. Thirteen.

She was wearing a pair of blue jeans and a large sweater. Her hair pulled out of her face. She looked squeaky clean.

She only forgave us when we explained about Batiste and how happy he looked going off with his mom.

After we got clothes, we were each given a backpack.

The backpacks were white, with no logo at all. They had inside them a little Dopp kit, with a toothbrush, toothpaste, a razor, and soap. Also some basic first aid stuff – wound wash, Band-Aids, antibiotic ointment, a foil pack of pain pills.

All the food vendors: Wolfgang's, Burger King, Pizza Shack,

etc. had been turned into mess halls. The food was the same (from what I've been told) for every meal. Oatmeal for breakfast, with fruit, if you got there early enough. Beef stew for lunch (no one there was a vegetarian, I guess). Chicken stew for dinner. Rice on the side. Oranges for dessert. Sometimes apples.

There were boxes and boxes of bottled water to drink.

We stood there, a little lost. People bustled around in every direction.

I scanned the faces passing by, hoping to see one of our parents. If I could find them in time, they'd make someone go back for you.

But it was useless. There were thousands of people milling and pushing past.

'Look!' Sahalia said. She pointed up to a big board.

It had numbers listed in batches, along with hours of departures and gate information. Like 7,989–8,425 Gate B7 11:45 a.m.

Our numbers weren't even on the board yet.

'Let's get food,' Niko said. He was carrying Max on his back, piggyback style. 'Then I'm going to get you guys to the gate.'

'What are you going to do then?' Sahalia asked, sounding edgy.

'I'm going to go find someone and organize a rescue.'

I looked at Niko. I couldn't read any emotion on his face.

'Do you mean it?' I said.

'Of course.'

Before I could get excited, Max threw up. It was pure bile – a weird neon-green colour. His eyes rolled in the back of his head and he started to shake.

People around us screamed and made a commotion.

A big guy helped Niko to get Max down onto the ground but Max

was still shuddering and shaking.

'We need a medic!' someone shouted. 'We need a medic here!'

Grown-ups were all over us now, and we were getting pushed apart.

'Clear back!' shouted a woman. 'Clear BACK!'

She was a reservist – we'd seen lots of them on the inside of the airport. Their uniforms were a little different from the regular Army soldiers.

She pushed the adults back with one arm and with the other she escorted an overweight medic. He had a satchel full of medical supplies and a red cross painted on his uniform.

He removed a syringe of some kind and shot it into Max's arm and the quaking stopped.

'He's going to be okay,' the medic said.

'All right, you heard him. The boy's going to be fine. Everyone get to your gates. We need to get you out of here as soon as possible, folks! This is an evacuation, not a sideshow!' the reservist bellowed.

She had grey hair pulled back in a bun and was much shorter than the other soldier, but she was clearly the boss. She wore camouflage fatigues and had the three bars of a sergeant on her arm.

Then Ulysses asked something in his heavy accent.

His eyes were wide and he was pointing at the lady.

I couldn't believe what he was saying and I turned to see the lady reservist's face.

Ulysses repeated, 'Mrs Wooly?'

And it was.

It was Mrs Wooly, Dean!

It said it right there on her uniform: WOOLY.

She looked at Ulysses blankly for a moment. Her face just wiped clean of all emotion and then she shouted, 'Ulysses Dominquez?'

She looked at him, at Niko, at me and Max and Sahalia, and then she gave a kind of screech. A giant, triumphant screech!

And she hugged Sahalia, nearly lifting her off the ground. And then she hugged me and Niko and Ulysses.

'These are my kids, Goldsmith!' she shouted to the medic. 'These are the ones I've been telling you about!'

'No kidding,' he said, already at work bandaging Max's feet. 'Really? From Monument?!'

Ulysses got down next to Max and was trying to wake him up, to show him we'd found Mrs Wooly.

Max's eyes fluttered open.

'Look!' Ulysses crowed. 'Mrs Wooly!'

Max looked up at her. He started to cry. 'Why didn't you come for us?'

'Oh, Max, I tried,' she said.

'We waited and waited!' Max wailed.

Mrs Wooly pressed her hand to Max's forehead.

'I tried to come for you, buddy. I put in a request with my CO but that didn't look like it was going to pan out. So I've been asking every chopper pilot I meet if he would just sneak me over to go and look for you but none of them would do it for me.'

The medic finished wrapping Max's feet. He patted Mrs Wooly on the shoulder and headed off.

Sahalia was looking at Mrs Wooly with an emotion I couldn't read. Anger? Contempt?

'We needed you!' Sahalia said accusingly. 'We lost . . . we lost

0 MILES

people. Brayden got shot! If you had come . . .' She couldn't finish the sentence, but she didn't really need to.

Mrs Wooly pushed some hair out of Sahalia's face. She took Sahalia's hand in hers.

'Oh, Sahalia, I'm so sorry. I'm so sorry that whatever happened happened. It must have been horrible, honey,' she said in her gravelly voice.

'I made it to the high school and I was trying to get a hold of a bus to come for you guys and there was this little kind of riot there and then this alert came over the radio. I had to report for duty. That's how it is for us. When called to serve, we gotta serve. But I swear to you I've spent every moment trying to figure out how to get you rescued. But none of that matters. You're here. You made it.'

'Niko said you were coming in a Kia minivan,' Max said.

'A Kia?! No way, honey. I only drive Subarus. And school buses.' She rustled Max's hair. 'You should see the Airbuses, kids. A whole fleet of A380s. Loading and flying and loading and flying. You'll be on the next one out. I'm going to see to that!'

'Are we going to Alaska?' Max asked.

'But Mrs Wooly—' I said.

'You might,' she said. 'But they're going all over. Lots of flights to Canada. Vancouver, Ottawa, BC.'

'But Mrs Wooly—' Niko tried to interrupt.

'They got hit much less hard than we did and have been really amazing. This time tomorrow, you guys will be safe. Maybe somewhere sunny even.'

Max and Ulysses looked at each other and smiled.

'But Mrs Wooly!' I yelled. 'We have to go back.'

'Go back?' she said, puzzled.

'Dean and Astrid and Chloe and Caroline and Henry are still at the store,' I said.

She went white and said, 'Hell.'

Mrs Wooly grabbed the first reservist she saw. He was a young guy, chewing gum, and had a long neck and the kind of head that bobs a lot. She took him off to the side and gave him a bunch of directions. She looked serious. He looked half-irritated, half-amused.

Then she came back to us with the guy.

'Kids, this is Frank. He's going to get you on the next plane out of here.'

'What?' I said. 'No!'

'I'm going to do the best I can to get your brother and the others. But look,' she told us, leaning in closer. 'You gotta get out of here now. It may not be safe for much longer.'

'What do you mean?' Sahalia asked.

'What's happening?' Niko said.

'Just go with Frank!' Mrs Wooly ordered. 'He'll get you guys on the next plane out of here. I have to go!'

And with that she started running – running away from us.

Frank grabbed a wheelchair for Max and deposited him in it.

'Follow me, squirts,' he said.

He went and looked at the call-board and said, 'Gate A-40,' and then, 'All right, let's get this done.'

Niko looked pissed. Sahalia looked scared. And I was just puzzled.

0 MILES

We all just followed along as Frank led us to the elevator and then down to the shuttle train.

My mind was catching up to the moment.

What had she meant, it might not be safe for much longer?

We waited on the shuttle platform. I guess I was in a daze.

A shuttle came and I tried to get on.

Frank pulled me back.

'Look, dummy!' he said, pointing to a sign that read: RESTRICTED! MILITARY PERSONNEL ONLY.

The soldiers in the car were all talking to one another and asking one another questions and checking their gear. They were excited – anxious – stirred up about something. But what?

Our shuttle came and Frank pushed his way in with Max's wheelchair. The rest of us jammed in near them.

I asked Frank, 'What did Mrs Wooly mean, it's not safe?'

'Can't tell you,' he said. 'Sorry, kid.'

Niko caught my eye.

'He probably doesn't know,' Niko said dismissively. 'He probably doesn't have security clearance.'

'What do you know about the military?' Frank snorted.

'Are reservists even in the military?' I asked. 'You're not even in the Army.'

'We are too in the Army!' Frank protested.

'Then why don't they tell you what's going on?' Niko taunted.

'Operation Phoenix,' Frank said, indignant. 'A battery of thermobaric bombs. Detonation sites all over NORAD and Colorado Springs.'

'They're going to burn the air,' Niko gasped.

'Yeah! Big-time!' Frank clucked. 'Gotta try to incinerate the compounds 'cause they're starting to spread. It's called thermal oxidation, you little twits.'

'What are you guys talking about?' Sahalia asked.

'Nothing you need to know, missy,' Frank said.

He thought he was so cool because he'd shocked us into silence.

At the gate a soldier was making an announcement over a megaphone.

'Ladies and gentlemen, we will now begin boarding. Please make one long line right here. Seating is open. Keep families together. No pushing or shoving.'

We got in line.

Ulysses and Max were playing around with the wheelchair, Ulysses tilting Max back and Max laughing like crazy.

'You can leave us now, if you want,' Niko told Frank. Niko made himself look like he thought Frank was a big shot, somehow. 'I mean, you must have a lot to do . . .'

'Yeah, I do,' Frank muttered, cracking his neck. 'I'm not here to babysit.'

'We can get on the plane ourselves,' I said.

'All right then,' Frank agreed. 'Good luck, squirts.' And he took off.

'I'm not going,' I whispered to Niko as soon as Frank was out of earshot. 'I'm going to find Mrs Wooly and help her organize the rescue.'

Niko didn't say anything.

'If you think about it,' I continued, 'one woman trying to get a

0 MILES

rescue operation going for some kids – who cares? But if I'm there . . . I'm the brother. I'm a kid. It will, I don't know, *move* people.'

Niko immediately turned to Sahalia.

'No,' she said.

'Get the kids on the plane,' he said. 'We will find you.'

'No!' she protested. 'We don't even know where this plane is going!'

'We'll find you,' I told her. 'I swear it! I swear to you we'll find you!'

She crushed me to her in a hug. Then she hugged Niko, too.

'Don't let this be the last time I see you,' she said to me.

'I won't,' I answered.

Sahalia turned to Niko and hugged him tight.

'Thank you,' she said to him. 'I'm sorry for what a jerk I was sometimes. You saved my life. You saved it a dozen times. That's the truth.'

Then she turned to Max and Ulysses. They were still messing around with the wheelchair.

'Come on, boys, it's time for us to get on the plane.'

She pushed Max's chair forward, edging through the people in front of her.

Ulysses looked back at us, confused at why we weren't coming, and I heard Max holler, 'Wait! What?'

'Come on,' Niko told me, and we started running.

24 DEAN

PAYTON LOOKED UP AT Astrid. Hi mouth fell open and he was shocked. I used that moment to get my hand on his hand, on the gun. I pushed the gun and his hand away from me. And then Payton looked back down at me and snarled.

Our hands were both on the gun and I was flat on my back on the table. I got my leg up and kicked him, as hard as I could, and I held on tight to the gun.

And I shot, as he stumbled back, and it hit him.

I didn't mean to and I did mean to and I shot him right in the chest.

Payton fell to the floor. His mouth was open and he was looking at me with a horrible expression on his face.

An expression of confusion.

'Jesus Christ!' Jimmy screamed. 'You killed him!'

225

DAY 15

Jimmy backed away from me.

Astrid turned the chainsaw off.

I sat up. My hands shaking. I had just shot Payton.

Caroline and Henry started shrieking. I didn't want them to see Payton. I didn't want them to have seen me shoot him but I couldn't take it back. His blood was pooling out around him.

I couldn't stop looking at him.

'Hey!' Astrid said. I jerked my head away to look at her.

'You saved us. Remember that.'

'Oh, Dean!' Caroline cried. I stumbled toward them. She and Henry came forward and hugged me.

The twins talked at the same time, asking me if I was okay and telling me how scared they had been and asking if Payton was really dead.

Jake groaned from where he lay on the floor.

Astrid took a step forward towards him, but Jimmy thought she was coming for him.

'Please, p-p-please,' he begged. 'Don't kill me.'

'I have a better idea,' said Chloe, stepping out from behind Astrid.

She stomped over to the juice and held up the bottle. 'Drink!'

'I don't want to die!' Jimmy sobbed.

'Oh, for Pete's sake,' Chloe snapped, 'it's not poison in there. Just sleeping pills.'

Jimmy Doll Hands brought the bottle to his lips and drank it.

'All of it,' Astrid said.

And so he chugged it.

'What should I do with this one?' Astrid said with contempt.

She still had Anna by the hair.

'Make her drink!' Chloe snarled.

'No,' I said. 'We'll just tie her up.'

'She should drink, the little rat!'

'For Christ's sake, I don't know the dosage!' I shouted.

'We'll just tie her up!'

Chloe looked chastened.

'This isn't a game,' I yelled. 'These are people's lives.'

And a stupid sob came up in my chest, just as Jimmy Doll Hands sank to the floor.

Anna said nothing as we tied her hands. Not even 'Thank you for not drugging me.' It was almost like we were boring her. She just wandered over to Payton and stood staring down at him.

I felt bad for her. The girl was clearly psychotic.

After Anna's hands were bound, Astrid and I tried to wake up Jake.

He obviously had retained some of the sleeping pill 'juice' before he puked.

'I know! I know!' Henry volunteered. 'When our mom needs to stay awake when she's driving she has an energy drink!'

'Sure, find one,' I said.

It was okay. We had time to try it, even if it was a

DAY 15

dumb, little kid kind of a solution.

The cadets would sleep for at least eight hours. We were out of danger. But we did have to figure out what to do with them.

Astrid sat, looking at Jake's face.

She was studying it. She must have felt me looking at her, because she looked up.

'That was very brave, Dean,' she said to me.

'No,' I said. 'I was scared.'

'That doesn't mean it wasn't brave,' she said.

The thought of Payton's face after I'd shot him didn't make me feel brave at all. It made me want to throw up. It made me feel low and dirty and ashamed.

'What do we do now? What do we do with them?' I asked her.

Henry and Caroline came back with the drink.

I opened Jake's mouth and tried to pour the contents of the little vial in.

Jake choked and sputtered. I think it was more the sensation of drowning that woke him than the ingredients of the drink, but who cared.

'I say we drag them up onto the roof and lock them out,' Astrid said. 'But we keep their guns.'

25 ALEX

'RESTRICTED AREA, BOYS!' A soldier said, barring us from getting on the military shuttle.

'Our mom's in the Air Force,' Niko lied. 'She told us to come and find her if Operation Phoenix was a go!'

'Oh, uh, okay,' the soldier grumbled, letting us past.

We slipped onto the shuttle and the doors closed right behind us.

The soldiers around us paid no attention to us. Some of them were Air Force, some were Army. Some were Marines, I guess. It was chaotic.

The shuttle opened up into the C terminal. They had it dedicated to military flights.

Through the big glass bays, where you'd usually see a Jet Blue 757, ready to take people to NY or Atlanta or wherever, there were military jets, helicopters in all different models, and giant Airbuses

0 MILES

painted combat colours. At several of the gates, they had small decontamination tents. I guess if anyone needed to come back in, they got sprayed down here. There were also bins with clothing and gear near the entrances from the decontamination tents.

Pilots and soldiers were swarming purposefully every which way. Many were wearing flight suits with air masks. Niko and I were the only two people who didn't seem to know exactly where we were supposed to go.

'Hey!' said a voice, headed for us.

'Come on,' Niko said, and we walked as fast as we could away from whoever it was who had noticed us.

'You kids!'

We searched frantically for any sign of Mrs Wooly.

'You're Wooly's kids!'

We turned then.

It was Goldsmith, the medic.

'What are you guys doing here? I thought Wooly was putting you on a plane!'

'We need to find her,' I told him.

'Now is not the time!' he said. 'They moved the whole operation up.'

'It's life or death,' Niko pleaded, grabbing his arm. 'Please, help us! Do you know where she is?'

'Last I saw she was near gate 33.' Goldsmith pointed. 'You better hurry!'

We had a direction now and we ran, darting into the stream of pilots and soldiers.

'There!' Niko said, pointing.

We came close and heard her scolding, 'Christopher Caldwell,

I've known you since you were a kid! You're gonna get in that chopper and you're gonna run me over there!'

'No, Wooly. I said no, for God's sake. I got orders. Orders!'

'They're a bunch of kids, Caldwell, and they're gonna be burned to a crisp. A bunch of kids you could save. Think about it. They'll give you a medal!'

'It's a suicide mission. The answer's no!'

'Please, mister.' I went close and grabbed his arm. 'It's my brother, Dean. My big brother and he's a great big brother and he's counting on us!'

'Alex, Niko! What are you doing here? For Christ's sake, you should be halfway to Vancouver!' Mrs Wooly looked mad as hell.

'We can't go without the others,' Niko argued. 'We just can't!'

'You kids go get on a godforsaken plane. I'll take care of this.'

'Good luck, Wooly,' said Caldwell, and he turned and left.

'They're little kids,' I screamed after him. 'Two teenagers and an eight year old and five-year-old twins! Five-year-old twins! And we came all the way from Monument! Can't you help us?'

Then there was a pilot coming at me wearing an air mask, all suited up to go. He grabbed me hard, I mean really hard, and he said, his voice all electronic, 'What twins in Monument?'

And I opened my mouth to tell him but he ripped off his air mask and I saw his face.

It was Mr McKinley. Our neighbour.

It was Mr McKinley, Dean.

Henry and Caroline's *dad*.

'Where are they?' Mr McKinley asked.

'They're at the Greenway, in Monument,' Niko said. 'We left

0 MILES

them three days ago.'

We hurried along with him.

'What's the best way in?' he asked us.

'We should land on the roof,' Niko told him. 'There's a hatch and it's easy to open from the inside.'

'There's no "we",' Mr McKinley said. Captain, I mean. 'I'm going alone.'

'What?' I screeched. 'We're going, too.'

'Yeah!' Niko shouted.

'You kids cannot go,' Mrs Wooly yelled. 'No way!'

'You need us!' Niko insisted. 'We know how to get into the store.'

'We're probably going to die,' Captain McKinley growled at us.

'No,' I told him. 'We're going to make it. We're going to save them!'

I knew it, in my gut.

Captain McKinley nodded and wiped his eyes and gave me a clap on the shoulder.

'Grab masks,' he said, nodding to some canvas bins near the gate. 'Get good ones.'

'All right, Jesus,' Mrs Wooly said. 'I'll suit up.'

'We don't need you,' Captain McKinley said. 'Stay here. Help with the evac.'

'I should come,' she said.

'That's an order!'

'But—'

Captain McKinley grabbed her by the front of her uniform.

'You want to help, try to get up to the control tower and get us cleared for takeoff so they don't shoot us out of the sky for deserting!'

'Okay,' Mrs Wooly said, shaken. 'Will do.'

She hugged me and Niko, and took off at a run.

Niko and I rummaged through the bin, looking for good masks. Captain McKinley came back with flight jumpers for me and Niko.

'Airtight,' he said. 'Get these on. They're dropping bombs over NORAD in 20 minutes. We'll have another 5 to 7 minutes after that before they level Monument. If we're going, we're going now.'

'How long will it take us to get there?' I asked as Niko struggled into his suit.

'In a Wildcat, at full throttle – 16 minutes.'

'We're going to make it!' I said.

Captain McKinley's helicopter looked fast. I got to sit up front with him. Niko had to sit in the back.

Captain McKinley plugged a cord into his face mask and pointed for me to do the same. It was a jack into the communication system. I could hear the dispatchers going crazy giving directions to the planes and helicopters.

Captain McKinley reached over and across me, flipping switches all over the place. The engine roared to life and the propellers started. I was glad for the noise-cancellation headphones built into the air mask – it was *loud!*

'Wildcat 185, you are not cleared for takeoff! Repeat, you are not cleared!'

Mrs Wooly had not made it! She hadn't made it in time!

'Tower, this is Captain McKinley, going on a rescue mission.'

233

0 MILES

'McKinley,' shouted the voice on the headset, 'what the hell are you doing? You are *not* cleared!'

'Sorry, Tower, it can't be helped.'

'Stand down, Wildcat 185, we will open fire—'

'It's my kids, Tower. They're alive. They're in the Phoenix zone and I'm going for them.'

'Jesus, McKinley ...'

In the background, other voices were shouting directions to all the other planes, clearing coordinates and assigning them for takeoff.

'Go get 'em, Hank,' the tower man said. 'God bless you. Wildcat 185, you are cleared.'

Then another voice added, 'Good luck, McKinley!'

And another, 'Go get your kids!'

Takeoff was bumpy.

'Visibility is limited,' Captain McKinley said to me. 'It's one hell of a weapon, the inkbomb. Lucky for us, though, we're flying one hell of an aircraft.'

He wheeled toward Monument and I held on and even though I am agnostic, I prayed.

26 DEAN

JAKE HAD A DIFFERENT opinion about what we should do.

'Look,' he argued. 'The bus is right outside and we know it runs! We should get out of here and go to Denver.'

'But the others could be coming here to rescue us!' I protested. 'Someone could be on the way.'

'Dean,' Jake said solemnly, 'Payton kicked them out of the bus. They were on foot. There's no way they made it.'

I didn't want him to be right. Maybe they were still out there. Maybe they had made it.

'But that doesn't mean we can't get to Denver,' Jake continued. 'We won't stop for anyone. And we have guns. Lots of guns!'

DAY 15

'I think Jake's right,' Astrid announced. 'We should try the bus.'

'What?' I asked, dumbfounded. 'Why? You were the one who made me stay!'

'I know it's a long shot but . . . maybe we could find the others. I mean, they're on foot . . .'

That made me think.

'At least, let's go look at the bus,' Jake pleaded. 'Just to see if it works!'

I was sick of hiding in that dark, cold store. A part of me wanted to get out in the air, even if the air killed me. But it was what Astrid said about my brother that put me over the edge.

Maybe we *could* find them.

We layered up.

'But we don't want to go outside!' Henry protested as I handed him his layers.

'It's scary out there,' Caroline continued.

'But you'll be with me this time,' I told them. 'And you know I would never let anything bad happen to you.'

They looked at each other, clearly unhappy about this plan.

'Are you two crazy? This is what we've been waiting for!' Chloe gushed. 'We're finally going to Denver! We're going to see our parents there and we'll all get rescued to Alaska. And Alaska is awesome! Get your stuff on! Hurry!'

'Okay.' Caroline gave in. 'We'll go.'

I left them and crossed to Astrid.

'We should take supplies,' I said. 'Food, water, lights, a tarp. If we're really going to try to make it.'

And then I remembered the backpacks I'd packed for Mr Appleton and Robbie.

I strode away from the group, into the storeroom. I looked around with my flashlight and there they were, behind a stack of packing crates.

I had thrown them back there after Robbie was shot. We had wanted it to look, to the little kids, like he had left so I'd hidden the backpacks there.

Astrid, Jake, and the kids came in, their headlamps bobbing all over the place. I prayed they wouldn't see the bodies. Or that if they did, they wouldn't understand what they were seeing.

'These are ready to go,' I said.

'Right on!' Jake replied.

Jake shouldered the heavier backpack. My shoulder still hurt plenty.

We had water, food, first aid stuff, some extra clothes (for full-grown men, but no matter), some flashlights. I couldn't remember what else had been packed.

And we climbed, single file, up the stairway to the hatch.

We were leaving our Greenway and we didn't have a moment to reflect or give gratitude to it. But of course, we were grateful.

'Wait!' Chloe shrieked through her mask. 'What about Luna?'

DAY 15

'Shoot!' Astrid said. 'She's still asleep! I'll get her. You guys go ahead.'

We climbed up.

It was dark up there.

Hard to see and breathe, with the mask on.

Hard to move, with all the layers on.

Henry clutched one of my hands, Caroline the other.

We made our way slowly over the pitted roof to the ladder.

'Dean, you go first,' Jake commanded. 'Then the kids, then Astrid and me.'

The rungs were slippery. It seemed like there was a fungus growing on the rungs' rubber foot treads.

But no one fell.

We waited for a moment at the bottom of the ladder, for Astrid. Then she came, wearing a new backpack.

'Where's Luna?' Chloe asked.

'Look,' Astrid said and turned around.

Luna's sleeping head stuck through the top of the backpack.

'This way,' Jake directed us.

And we followed him through the parking lot, away from the store.

I didn't try to talk, it was too hard with the masks.

I was holding Caroline's hand on one side and Henry's in the other. Astrid was holding Chloe's hand and Jake walked ahead of us.

Our little lights zigzagged the ground in front of us as

we trudged through the parking lot toward the bus.

The ground was slick in places. The grass in the little sections near the light poles was all dead. The hail-crushed cars were slimy with rust and this weird white foam.

No wonder Jake had come back and no wonder the cadets were so eager to be inside. It was creepy out in the dead world.

There was some of the feathery white foam growing on the tyres of the bus. Besides that, it looked fine.

We heard it first. A giant BOOM that made my ears ring.

I looked up. Over in the direction of NORAD, there was a giant fireball in the sky.

'Ooooh!' the kids yelled.

It did look far enough away to be fireworks.

Then, in the space where the fireball had been and in a circle around it, there was light. The sun had come in.

At first I thought, maybe this was good . . . Maybe they'd found a way to clean the air.

Two more explosions came. They were bombing the sky.

And then hot winds raced toward us over the ground and I knew that we were going to die.

DAY 15

ALEX

I SAW THE VILLAGE INN! I saw the 7-eleven! We were in Monument! The chopper was equipped with searchlights and there it all was, Monument, from above.

There was the roof of the Greenway – our roof! I was so happy. I just kept seeing Dean's face in my imagination. He was going to be so excited to see me!

The first bombs started exploding in the air above NORAD just as we touched down on the roof.

'We've got maybe five minutes!' Captain McKinley shouted.

We all scrambled out of our safety harnesses and raced across the scarred and hail-beaten roof to the hatch.

It was actually open, which was weird, but in the moment didn't seem weird, it just seemed terrific – getting in was the part I'd been worried about.

Niko and I rushed down the stairs.

'Dean! Astrid! We're here!' I shouted.

And then I saw the little girl.

The little blonde girl.

She was just standing over the bodies of Robbie and Mr Appleton, her wrists tied together.

'Little girl!' Captain McKinley called, coming down the stairs. 'We're here to rescue you! Where are the others?'

He didn't know. He didn't know who she was!

'You!' Niko shouted. 'How did you get here?'

Captain McKinley moved past us into the store, yelling for Henry and Caroline.

'Where are they?' I screamed at the girl. 'You tell me! You tell me right now!'

She was crying. I was crying.

'They left!' the girl said. 'They went off the roof. They killed my uncle Payton and they left!'

Inside I could hear Captain McKinley calling, 'Henry! Caroline!'

'Captain McKinley!' I screamed.

He came running.

'What is it? Where are they?'

BOOM came the sound of another bomb exploding over NORAD.

'They're gone,' I sobbed. 'They left the store!'

His face fell then. It went all grey.

'Right. Of course,' he said. Hard like a stone.

'I'm sorry!' I cried.

'Let's move out.'

69 MILES

DEAN

JAKE WAS IN THE bus, trying to get it to go. But the wheels wouldn't turn through the white stuff. They were disintegrated or something.

Astrid was next to me, the children huddled at our sides.

We would watch the bombs until they took us. That seemed to be the right plan.

Each detonation shook us and each detonation punched a hole in the sky. They were coming closer.

The light streamed in, in those pure, straight beams. 'God light' was what my mom had called it.

I thought of my mom and my dad and Alex, and I was full of love for them.

I drew Astrid to me. Astrid was so beautiful in her gas mask and all her layers and the little kids, too, and Jake

– now standing on the steps of the bus, his chest heaving, his head thrown back to look at the firebombs – was beautiful, too. And I thought of how perfect we all were at that moment. And had always been.

I was ready to die and then Chloe grabbed my arm and pointed back toward the store.

I turned and saw – there was a helicopter on the roof.

I turned to Astrid.

'Run!' I shouted.

DAY 15

ALEX

T HE SKY HAD HOLES in it. The air was hot and windy and it battered us as we crossed the roof.

'Get in the chopper!' Captain McKinley yelled to us.

The stupid blonde girl was getting rescued. She, who deserved it least of all.

Niko gave her a boost into the back. Her hands were tied so she couldn't climb.

Captain McKinley and I got in the cockpit. He clicked on the switches and pressed buttons, like he had done before, but now he was like a robot. It was his training, doing the preparations – the man was gone.

He flipped a switch and said, over the intercom, 'Be sure you're strapped in, back there.'

Let her not be strapped in, I thought to myself, let her fall out and die.

DEAN

THE CHOPPER STARTED TO lift!

They were leaving without us!

The explosions were closer now, coming more frequently. Every few seconds, we were thrown off our feet. It was like trying to run in a bouncy house.

I tore off my mask. I could use the O energy to run faster.

And I felt it, the surge, and I ran. I ran for it with everything I had.

ALEX

CAPTAIN MCKINLEY PUSHED UP on the control stick and the helicopter rose in the air. The air from the bombs rocked and buffeted the helicopter. He had to struggle with all his might to get it to lift.

But he did.

And we started off the roof against a steady *BOOM*, *BOOM*, *BOOM*.

DEAN

VAULTED UP THE LADDER, four runs at a time. I pulled myself onto the roof. Shouted, 'Alex!' I yelled with all my might, 'Alex!'

ALEX

I N A BOMB BLAST I saw a figure on the edge of the roof. He was running at us.

'Look!' I shouted. 'It's my brother. It's Dean!'

He was on the roof!

'What?' Captain McKinley shouted.

I grabbed his shoulder and pointed.

'That is my brother, Dean!'

'Copy. Setting down. Brace yourself!' Captain McKinley shouted, wrestling the control stick. He struggled to set the helicopter back down.

Dean came running to the chopper and I pushed the door open and fell out to the roof and then we were hugging!

'Dean! Dean! I found you.'

Then my brother put his head back and roared.

DEAN

I FOUGHT AGAINST THE COMPOUNDS. I tried to stay sane.

Niko tackled me, holding me down, and Alex took off his air mask and put it over me.

By then, Astrid and the kids and Jake were climbing onto the roof.

ALEX

'GET IN NOW!' CAPTAIN McKinley shouted.
    No time for hellos.
He literally threw his kids in the back of the chopper.
BOOM, *BOOM*, *BOOM*, the bombs were getting closer.

DEAN

ASTRID FUMBLED TO STRAP the kids in.

Niko shoved me into a seat and strapped me down.

I was trying to breathe. Trying to become human again.

'Good to see you, Dean,' Niko said. His voice came digitally right into my Army air mask, right in my ear.

Alex made his way to me, crawling over the others.

'We got you,' my brother said. 'We got you!'

ALEX

'HOLD ON!' CAPTAIN McKINLEY shouted. He lifted the helicopter back into the air.

I clicked into the seat next to Dean as *BOOM!* Searing winds hit us.

Captain McKinley wrestled the control stick, battling the winds for command of the helicopter.

BOOM! Another explosion to the right of us. The hot winds almost dashed us back down but he pulled up, up, up.

And then we were racing into the dark air. We were ahead of the bombs then and we got away from there, up into the black sky that was splintering now, shot through with sunlight and fire. And I held my brother's hand.

EPILOGUE
DEAN

WE DESERVE A HAPPY ending. All of us do. And I think we're going to get it. But I'm not exactly sure yet.

We're lucky to be here in Quilchena. Yes, we sleep in rows on cots in giant tents. Yes, armed guards patrol the perimeter. And yes, we have next to no contact with the outside world. But some of the American containment camps are much worse.

We hear stories of refugees being locked in prisons and denied all rights. There are some crazy rumours floating around about medical experiments being performed on O types. The Canadians at least treat us like human beings. They're polite and everything.

I feel bad for the poor Canadians. They had no idea

DAY 31

what they were in for when they allowed refugees to be air-lifted here.

It turns out that the survivors of the Four Corners disaster, as they're calling it on the news, are violent and unstable.

The first refugees they airlifted to Calgary and Vancouver started leaving the temporary housing and tearing through towns and cities – looting and rioting.

Now they have us all collected in containment camps and they're negotiating with the American government to see what will happen to us. The Canadians should never have taken us in. Alex has a theory that they felt partially responsible for the chemical weapons programme at NORAD because it's a joint venture between the US and Canada.

It's one p.m., and normally at this time, all the refugees gather in the dining hall. After lunch, they let us watch TV for one hour. Any more than an hour, they've found that the refugees get too hostile and shaken up.

There are a few mini-tabs being passed around, but there's less interest in them than you might think.

Alex got ahold of one and discovered that all the data's gone. All our e-mails. Our photos. Texts. Contacts. Accounts. It's all gone and we have no way to find our parents, because their accounts are gone, too.

It's creepy being online – a few stupid sites are up, but mostly there are missing pages and endless redirects. It's like the network has been struck with amnesia.

Alex has set up new accounts for us. If our parents are

out there, they will find us. I have to believe that.

In the meantime, at two p.m., the guards post the most recent refugee listings and we all pour over the lists, searching for the names of the people we've lost.

They're listed by zip code and then alphabetically.

I keep praying to see our parents: 80132 Grieder, James. Or 80132 Grieder, Leslie. But so far nothing.

No sign of Heyman, Lori, either. Or any of Astrid's younger siblings.

Ulysses, incredibly, found his whole family. And they have agreed to legally adopt Max if his parents don't show up. Max lives with them now and he loves it. Somehow, I feel certain that the Dominguez family will give him a more traditional and morally sound upbringing than Max's biological parents.

They are in Tent G, which is all families with young children.

Mrs McKinley lives there with the twins. The scene when Captain McKinley brought Caroline and Henry to their mom was joyous and heartbreaking and made everything – *everything* – worth it.

(Astrid reminds me of it every time I wake up shouting in the night. I still see Payton's face after I shot him. And the pallet loader guy I cut to pieces.)

Captain McKinley had to return to duty. Mrs McKinley took Chloe and Luna in out of the goodness of her heart. If we had to have Chloe with us in Tent J, I think I'd go nuts.

Mrs McKinley and the kids sometimes take Luna on

DAY 31

rounds through the infirmary. Luna has taken to the role of therapy dog like a pro. When people hold our face-licking, tail-wagging Luna and hear the story of how she got rescued, all the way from Monument, it seems to give them hope. Luna has sort of become the Quilchena mascot and no one is more proud of that than Chloe, who grooms Luna incessantly and walks her about eight times a day.

Captain McKinley told us he saw Mrs Wooly at the Fort Lewis-McChord Air Force Base. Apparently when she saw him, she was so happy that he was alive and that we'd made it out safely that she first kissed him on the mouth and then insisted on buying him and everyone else in the canteen drinks all night long. She drank them all under the table, of course.

I can't believe Mrs Wooly made it. Hearing about the moment when Ulysses spotted her at DIA is one of my favourite parts of the story. Captain McKinley says she's trying to get leave to come and visit us.

Alex, Astrid, Sahalia, Niko, and I live in Tent J. Tent J is basically for orphans age 8–17, but since I get to be with Alex and Astrid and Niko, I don't feel like an orphan at all.

Today we're not at the listings. Today we're having a party.

Mrs McKinley has made a picnic and requested permission for us all to go out on the community outdoor area on Hole 3. Everyone else is at the listings, so we have the whole green to ourselves.

It's the twins' birthday and they're turning six.

It's a beautiful day. There's a pond on this hole – a water feature, I guess they call it. And behind it are trees blazing in gold and orange and chestnut brown. This is a very nice golf club here, that they've turned into a prison for us.

Mrs McKinley has laid out a bedsheet as a picnic blanket and has clearly been saving her food and bartering so there can be treats for the kids. There's a bag of potato chips (everyone is careful to only take one or two) AND a bag of cheese doodles AND somehow, she's wrangled a package of chocolate-covered doughnuts. Pretty impressive.

Caroline and Henry are playing with their present – a soccer ball. Ulysses and Chloe join and they start playing a little game with two of Ulysses's older brothers serving as goalies. Luna is running and barking and generally getting in the way.

The grown-ups sit on the parched grass and watch the game.

This feels almost like real life again.

Max is watching from a very comfortable position on the generous lap of Mrs Dominguez. I can tell he'd like to join in, but his feet still aren't a hundred percent yet. Mrs Dominguez takes him to the clinic and waits in the long queue with him every day so he can be seen. She's been doing that with him for the two weeks since we got here.

Mrs Dominguez is combing Max's hair with her fingers

DAY 31

and that cowlick of his just springs up every time. I bet she never thought she'd be the mother of a towhead.

'Where'd they get the ball, do you think?' Astrid says as she comes to stand beside me.

She puts her arm around my waist and I draw her into me.

Think I've gotten used to having her as my girlfriend? I haven't.

She glows in the sun. I don't know whether it's the pregnancy or if it's just that I love her so stupidly much, but every time she comes near me, I basically have to shade my eyes, she's so bright and beautiful.

But I'm not so shy around her anymore, which is good, and I don't try to pretend to be anything I'm not.

I figure she knows who I am by now.

'The Captain must have smuggled it in,' I say, nodding toward the ball. 'No way Mrs McKinley could have bartered for it in here.'

Alex and Sahalia are sitting on the grass. They're too far away for me to hear what they're talking about, but Alex says something that makes Sahalia roll her eyes and punch him in the shoulder. Then they both laugh.

It's weird. I don't know what happened between them on the road. It's not like they're a couple, but they hang out almost every day. Sahalia watches Alex fix electronics that people bring to him and Alex hangs out while Sahalia roots through the charity bins for clothes. Her birthday's coming up too and Alex has been bartering to get her a pair of black biker boots she's coveting.

Right now Sahalia's wearing white painter's coveralls rolled up to the knee, with the sleeves cut off and a red bandanna tied around her waist.

She's got flair, all right.

I feel Astrid go tense.

It's Jake. Jake's coming up the faded green hill with his dad.

He and his dad found each other the first day we arrived.

I'm jealous of him (because of his dad).

But that's okay, because he's jealous of me, too (because of Astrid).

We give each other a wide berth.

'Hey, y'all,' Jake calls out.

'Uncle Jake! Uncle Jake!' the kids screech and yell. They abandon their game and run to him, tackling him. They all roll down the hill together in a big dog pile.

(You'd think Max would be feeling left out, but no, he just buries himself deeper into Mrs Dominguez's willing arms and lets himself be mothered and fussed over.)

'Now, where'd I put that present?' Jake says to the kids. He tickles Henry and then Caroline. "Is it under your neck? Maybe it's here in your armpit!' The kids are all laughing.

Jake pulls out a package of Gummi bears and the kids go nuts. Gummi bears were no big deal back at the Greenway, where we had dozens of bags of them, but now that they're scarce, the kids covet them.

'He's doing better,' Astrid says.

DAY 31

'Yup,' I say.

I don't tell her what Alex told me – Jake is on antidepressants and seeing a counsellor.

Jake can tell her himself. They talk sometimes. She tries to explain why she chose me over him. He probably tries to persuade her to get back together with him.

But that's not going to happen. Our plan is that the baby will call Jake 'Daddy' and will call me 'Dean' and that's fine with me. I don't need the title. I want the position.

'Hey! Hey, everyone,' Mrs McKinley sings. 'Is everyone here?'

'Where's Niko?' Astrid asks me.

'Probably at the listings,' I say.

Niko's the one who's doing the worst out of all of us. He wanders around, not really engaging with anyone. He's not been able to find any word of anyone from his family.

And he's still mourning Josie.

He sketches sometimes, but he won't show anyone the drawings.

'Gather around, please,' Mrs McKinley calls to us.

Mrs McKinley has put two birthday candles in the centre of two of the tiny doughnuts. They share one thin paper plate.

Before she lights them, Mrs McKinley pushes her long auburn hair out of her eyes. She looks just like the twins – wall-to-wall freckles, light blue-green eyes. She especially looks like them when she smiles and her eyes crinkle up in the corners.

'I just want to say thank you, for taking care of my babies. I will never stop being grateful to you kids. I owe you . . . I owe you everything,' and she stops because she's so choked up.

I don't know how we did it, actually. I don't know how we managed to save them.

Alex and I take long walks during the outdoor period for Tent J. We do laps and we recount what happened to us in each other's absence. There's no older/younger between us anymore – we're equals now.

We talk about the future.

We can't believe we even have one.

Looking around our little circle, I wish that Niko was with us and I worry about him. I wish Brayden had made it. I will always regret the way that he died. And poor lost Josie – her last hours must have been horrible beyond what any of us could imagine.

I look at Mrs McKinley and her grinning twins.

I look at Sahalia, who is still, somehow, cooler than the rest of us, and Chloe, who is still, somehow, a brat.

And at the brothers, Ulysses and Max, standing with the rest of the Dominguez family. I wish Batiste could be here to stand with them, for he's also our family, but he's in Calgary, we think. I bet Batiste thinks about us all the time.

I look at Jake and his dad, who are going to be okay in the end, I think.

And at my brother, Alex, who I will never, ever leave again.

DAY 31

And the beautiful Astrid, who I would kill for, and already have.

The gratitude I feel swells up and tears come into my eyes. But that's okay, because as Henry and Caroline blow out their candles, everyone else is crying, too.

A figure is approaching over the hills and grass. It's Niko and he's running.

'Guys, guys!' he shouts, breathless. 'Look!'

He holds up the front section of a printed newspaper. Printed papers have made a comeback with the interruption of the Network. We all pull in close to see.

A headline reads: **CLOUDS OF WARFARE COMPOUNDS RUMORED ADRIFT**

Reading that gives me a pit of cold dread in my stomach.

But that's not what Niko's so excited about.

He points to another, smaller headline: **RIOTS AT UMO!**

The subheadline reads, **Refugees rise in rebellion at the University of Missouri containment camp**

Niko puts his finger on a full-colour picture.

It's an old guy being protected from a guard wielding a nightstick.

'It's Mr Scietto!' Alex yells.

And next to him, shielding Mario Scietto from the blow, is a girl with her hair up in two giraffe bumps.

It's Josie.

The girl in the picture is Josie!

'I'm going for her,' Niko says, eyes flashing between me and Jake and Alex.

'Who's coming?'

DAY 31

ACKNOWLEDGMENTS

I would like to thank my editor and publisher, Jean Feiwel, for her guidance and encouragement. Holly West, thank you for knowing this manuscript backward and forward and for all your wonderful ideas. I am so glad I have the two of you on my side. I must also thank Dave Barrett, the Executive Managing Editor, for his patience, and the fantastic copyeditor, Anne Heausler, for her work on this novel.

Thanks to my agent, Susanna Einstein, for her support and excellent advice. I also feel lucky to have Stephen Moore, Kim Stenton, and Sandy Hodgman on my team.

Rich Deas, you have a great vision for the art of this series. Thank you. And thanks to KB, April, and Katie, for designing the jackets and interior elements of the books. Karen Frangipane and Ksenia Winicki, thank you for helping to keep *Monument 14* at play in the digital realm.

The series owes much of its success to the efforts of Angus Killick, Elizabeth Fithian, Alison Verost, Kate Lied, Kathryn Little, and the rest of the excellent Macmillan Children's Group marketing and publicity departments. I have to say that touring with Allison, Kate, Elizabeth Mason, and Courtney Griffin was so outrageously fun, it's hard to believe it was legal. *Was it all legal?* I'm not entirely sure. That stuff in Pensacola was pretty dodgy.

I'd like to thank composer Paul Libman for writing music for the songs 'Get Up' and 'Leave Me Be,' both of which you can hear at emmylaybourne.com. Thanks to Ava Anderson for rocking the vocals and to Uri Djemal at MadPan studios for recording and engineering these songs so beautifully.

Mother/son critical feedback team Kristin and Andrew Bair worked their magic on *Sky on Fire*. Thank you both. I owe Elizabeth Harriman big-time for her help with the scene where Batiste and his mother are reunited. And thanks to Rita Arens and Scott Taylor for being excellent beta readers.

To Jen Pattap and Jeanette and Anthony LoPinto of the Threefold café – you guys have fed me, heart and soul, since I started on this series. Thank you.

My gratitude to my parents goes so far beyond what I could ever fit on this page. The same thing goes for how I feel about my husband, Greg, and our two children,

Elinor and Rex. A writer should be able to express these things, but I find myself overcome when I think about how fortunate I am to have you fine people to love.

Read on for a sneak peek of the exciting
Savage Drift.
Will Niko and Dean manage to rescue Josie?
Find out in May 2014 …

JOSIE

I KEEP TO MYSELF.

The Josie who took care of everyone – that girl's dead.

She was killed in an Aspen grove off the highway somewhere between Monument and Denver.

She was killed along with a deranged soldier.

I killed her when I killed the solider.

I am a girl with a rage inside that threatens to boil over every minute of the day.

All of us here are O types who were exposed. Some of us have been tipped into madness by the compounds.

It depends on how long you were exposed.

I was out there for more than two days.

* * *

I work on self-control every moment of the waking day. I have to be on guard against my own blood.

I see others allow it to take over. Fights erupt. Tempers flare over an unfriendly glance, a stubbed toe, a bad dream.

If someone gets really out of control, the guards lock them in the study rooms at Hawthorn.

If someone really, *really* loses it, sometimes the guards take them and they don't come back.

It makes it worse that we're just a little stronger than we were before. Tougher. The cycle of healing, a bit speeded up. Not so much you notice, but old ladies not using their canes. Pierced ear holes are closing up. More energy in the cells, is what the inmates say.

They call it the O advantage.

It's our only one.

The Type O Containment camp at Old Mizzou is a prison, not a shelter. The blisterers (Type A), the paranoid freaks (Type AB) and the people who've been made sterile (Type B), are at refugee camps where there's more freedom. More food. Clean clothes. TV.

But all of the people here at Mizzou have Type O blood and were exposed to the compounds. So the authorities decided we are all murderers (probably true – certainly is for me) and penned us in together. Even the little kids.

'Yes, Mario,' I say when he starts to grumble about how wrong it all is. 'It's unjust. Goes against our rights.'

But every time my fingers itch to bash some idiot's nose in, I suspect they were right to do it.

I remember my Gram talking about fevers. I remember her sitting on the edge of my bed, putting a clammy washcloth on my forehead.

'Gram,' I cried. 'My head hurts.'

I didn't say it aloud, but I was begging for Tylenol and she knew it.

'I could give you something, my baby girl, but then your fever would die, and fever's what makes you strong.'

I would cry, the tears themselves seemed boiling hot.

'A fever comes in and burns up your baby fat. It burns up the waste in your tissue. It moves you along in your development. Fevers are very good, darlin'. They make you invincible.'

Did I feel stronger afterwards? I did. I felt clean. I felt tough.

Gram made me feel like I was good through and through and I would never do wrong.

I'm glad Gram is long dead. I wouldn't want her to know me now. Because the O rage comes on like a fever but it burns up your soul. It makes your body strong and lulls your mind to sleep with bloodlust and you can recover from that. But after you kill, your soul buckles. It won't lie flat; like a warped frying pan, it sits on the burner and rattles, uneven.

* * *

You can never breathe the same way again because every breath is one you stole from corpses rotting in the ground, unburied, where you left them to bleed out.

As I understand it, the National Government brought us here, but the State of Missouri is running the camp. The locals don't want us released, but don't care to pay for us to be properly cared for either. And the National Government has been slow to provide for us.

The result: not enough guards, not enough food, not enough space, not enough medical care. And they won't let us out.

There were petitions circulating, when we first arrived. People trying to get the stable Os separated from the criminal ones. But the guards made life hard for the signature-gatherers.

Now we're all just waiting it out.

Every week a rumour drifts through the camp that we're to be released.

The hope is dangerous to me. It makes me care.

Q&A with Emmy Laybourne

What inspired you to write the *Monument 14* books?

I think the seed of the *Monument 14* series comes from two of my great loves: survivalist planning and superstores! I love to wander the aisles of superstores, checking out the goods and seeing how I would set up camp in the store, if I had to. And I've always enjoyed 'worst case scenario' thinking. It's the worrier in me, but I'm always thinking of how I will save my kids' lives if we're in some terrible crisis . . .

I put those together and there was the central idea of *Monument 14* – fourteen kids stranded in a superstore while civilization collapses.

What would be your dream cast if the Monument 14 books were made into movies?

I can happily, happily name a few names, but remember that within a year or two my suggestions may be irrelevant because young actors age themselves out of roles . . . With that in mind, here are my dream choices for some of the lead roles:

Dean – Graham Phillips (*The Good Wife* – he's so wonderful in it!)

Astrid – Brigit Mendler (*Good Luck Charlie* – she's ready for her first dramatic role)

Jake – Josh Hutcherson (a little movie we know as *The Hunger Games!*)

Niko – Jake T. Austin (*The Wizards of Waverly Place* – I know, a silly show, but I think Jake has the chops!)

Josie – China Anne McClain (*A.N.T. Farm* – another comic actress who will get the chance to do some real acting here)

Brayden – Sterling Beaumon (*Lost* – check out his photo. Whoa!)

Sahalia – Elle Fanning (*Super 8* – I was blown away by her performance in this movie!)

Alex – Joel Courtney (*Super 8* – the perfect Alex. Or Dean, in about three years!)

Payton – I'm a huge Zac Efron fan – wouldn't he make a terrifying Payton?

What songs would be on the *Sky On Fire* soundtrack?
The *Sky On Fire* soundtrack would be filled to the brim with Radiohead! It's what I listen to when I write. Their music is slightly futuristic-sounding, you can really sink your teeth into the lyrics and melody, and there's something slightly sinister going on at the same time.

Which character in the series do you most relate to?
Dean. Dean's my boy. I relate to the way he feels that he's an observer and slightly on the outskirts of the social structure, at least at the beginning of the series. That's certainly how I felt when I was his age. Dean is always trying to do the right thing – sometimes he succeeds, but not all the time. I identify with that, too.

Who would be at your dream dinner party?
Shakespeare. Bam. His name popped into my mind before I was even done reading the question. I know you're probably thinking, 'Everyone says Shakespeare'. That's because we have to. It's our imagination-ly duty to put Shakespeare at the top of the list of any and all time-travel-allowing invitation lists. Just accept it.

I'd also like to meet E. E. Cummings, American playwright Thorton Wilder, Jane Austen and the poet Emily Dickinson. (I will seat Jane and Emily together, of course.) Michelle and Barack Obama go on the guest list, absolutely. Then I'd add Anne Lamott, because I think she would consent to hold my hand and help me to calm down so I can stop grinning like a doofus and ask

Shakespeare some intelligent questions. Actually, you know what, I'm going to add my dear Shakespeare professor, Don Foster. He'll know what to ask. Lastly, my Mom and Dad, because they throw the best dinner parties in the world, and I will need the help of their considerable social graces to pull this thing off.

Is there a book you wish you had written?

Fire by Kristin Cashore. I absolutely love the world she has created with the *Graceling* series. Fire is a fantastic heroine – tough as nails, deeply flawed. And what a ride Cashore takes us on in each and every novel she writes! I have no idea if she plans to continue the series, but I never, ever want it to end . . .

What advice would you give to aspiring young writers?

If you're going to be an artist of any kind, you will need to learn how to turn off your internal critic when you are working. You cannot create and judge your work simultaneously. It just doesn't work that way.

For this reason, I'd recommend taking an improv class! When you are doing improv, you learn very quickly how to shut that internal critic off – or he shuts you down. You can also learn a lot about story structure and character development on your feet in front of an audience.

Where is your favourite place to write?

I work in a lovely little office with cream-coloured walls hung with lots of photographs and art. It sits right next to a cafe where they serve local, organic food and is a one-minute walk away from my kids' school. It is the perfect office for me – better than I ever could have dreamed!

Follow Emmy on Twitter: @emmylaybourne

Fourteen kids.
One superstore.
A million things
that go wrong ...

EMMY LAYBOURNE

MONUMENT

14

LOVE LUST
WAR RAGE

WHAT DOES IT TAKE
TO SURVIVE?

'Frighteningly real ... riveting' New York Times